PRESERVATION

VACCINATION NOVEL BOOK 3

PHILLIP TOMASSO

Dedication

This one is for my three amazing kids,

For my parents,

And for my family at 911 . . .

PROLOGUE

I hated clowns. Nothing about them worked for me. They painted expressions onto their faces with gobs of makeup; giant, exaggerated smiles or frowns; tears and eyebrow art. They sported honking Rudolph-red noses, oversized shoes, baggy hula-hooped pants and striped shirts with lapel-pinned flowers that sprayed water. There was also no forgetting the multi-colored afros, or horseshoe-shaped balding patterned wigs. This was funny? No. In fact it was scary; downright creepy and frightening.

Julie hired not one, but *two*, for Cash's birthday party. The kid was turning three. What did he know about clowns? Cash wouldn't even sit on Santa's lap.

Santa.

Please, *please* don't get me started on how horrifying and perpetually wrong it is for a giant fat man with an unkempt beard and red velvet suit to want kids sitting on his knee. To be fair, I might just be referring to department store Santas. *Ah, excuse me? You want my kid to sit on your lap and tell you secrets? I don't think so, you fucking pervert!*

That's just me, the kind of dad I was. Call me cheap and overprotective if you'd like. The money spent on clowns, and the time wasted in lines at malls, just didn't add up to me at times.

"Where's Cash?" Playing host was always a challenging and daunting task. The backyard was dressed up with colored coiled streamers that ran along branches of the Rose of Sharon that outlined the property, and if you squinted, it might have resembled a festive circus-like environment. Somehow, all I could focus on was the swarms of bees that loved those flowery tree-like bushes. The bees were freaking everywhere. It was impossible to enjoy eating outside with all of those bees. I wanted to rent a pavilion for the party. We still could have decorated, had the clowns and everything else, but we just would have been able to do it without all of the bees. Day after the party, I was taking the Rose of Sharon down. All of them. I kept thinking how nice it would be mowing the lawn and not having to run by the bushes every time just to avoid agitating the stinging insects.

The bouncy house in the center of the yard was like an inflatable red torture chamber. The ten foot high fortress was made up of rows of bulbous tube upon bulbous tube filled with air from a running air pump generator. That generator hummed, grind and stunk of gasoline. Kids disappeared inside through a Velcro sealed doorway, and we lost them. They were gone. They had vanished into a rubbery castle that shook as if it was in the midst of a constant earthquake. It bounced and bobbed, and threatened to deflate. The entire time sounds of kids screaming went ignored. Parents mingled, scooping out handful after handful of M&Ms, salted peanuts or quickly going stale potato chips from bowls spread out on tables covered in Dollar Store tablecloths that needed to be taped to the underside to keep from blowing away. No one paid any attention to the chaos erupting inside the bouncy house, no one.

"Where is Cash?" I said, again, realizing that in order to be heard I needed to speak more loudly, and actually make physical contact placing my hands on my wife's shoulder in order to gain her attention.

"Cash? Oh, he's with my mother over in the high-chair," Julie said, and pointed with a nod of her head and using the tip of her nose like a finger. She carried a tray of fresh cut vegetables with homemade dipping sauce out of the house. It would be feverishly gobbled up. Family and friends were here to celebrate Cash's birthday, and brought gifts. Their reward for giving up precious time on a Saturday afternoon was being fed. They came hungry, always did. The bowls of junk, the trays of veggies were what made up the hors d'oeuvres. The coolers lining the back of the sun porch were filled with ice, beer and soda pop and would empty soon. It was okay, because we had a backup. We'd resort to two liter bottles stored in the fridge.

"You need any help?" I held the door open, even after she set the tray down on the closest table, since I knew she would be headed back inside. Serving guests was a chore that never ended. Pasta baked in the oven and salads needed dressing mixed. The kitchen table was in the process of transformation into a grand buffet line.

"We're set," she said. Call it old fashioned, but most of the females were inside prepping the main courses for lunch. No one told them they had to do it. I certainly never expected my wife to do the cooking. It's just the way things unfolded. Possibly, it had something to do with the fact I've been known to burn boxed mac and cheese.

I gave her a kiss. She smiled and ducked under my arm and went back into the house.

I spotted my mother-in-law standing by the highchair. Cash sat with his back toward me, his arms waved about up in the air.

"You know how to throw a party, McKinney." My brother-in-law clapped me on the back. I could smell beer and M&M's on his breath, despite the breeze outside. Couldn't fault him. It was a party. Beer was free. M&Ms were everywhere. Why not get lit. If it was his party, or anyone else's, for that matter, I would do the exact same thing.

My mother-in-law's mouth formed a giant "O" before she covered her face with both hands.

"Mom?" I started toward her, toward my son. Felt it in my stomach; a churning, a flip-flop. Something was wrong.

She stepped away from the highchair, took several steps backwards. I heard Cash cry. Despite the shouts that echoed out from the bouncy house; from the mood music that blared from a radio set in the kitchen window; from the fucking clowns doing lame magic tricks to their screaming-kid audience in front of me, I heard, distinctly, my son crying.

"Mom!" I said.

The first clown stepped in front of me with that goofy and eccentric smile, but I saw his real mouth camouflaged under a stoned application of red lipstick. He wasn't smiling. His lips weren't fooling me. And why did I give a shit that he was pulling yards of scarfs out of his sleeve? Why would anyone be impressed with that? Who the fuck would care?

I pushed him aside. The more steps I took toward my son, it seemed like the further away from him I was. I just couldn't get there, couldn't get to him.

The second clown was stooping forward. All I could hear at that moment was the squeaking scrape of balloons being twisted and tied into shapes. A horse, a dog, a crown, a sword. It wasn't an intentional hip-check, but I did send the clown stumbling forward and face first into a budding bush of Rose of Sharon. I heard the clown scream and watched him scramble backwards as bees stung his face and head. His swatting hands did nothing more than further irritate the bees. I did *not* laugh when he ran away from the bush into the bouncy house, fell flat on his back and gasped as the breath was knocked from his lungs. It was partly my fault, okay, but let's be serious, most of the blame for his lack of balance stemmed from his fucking huge Ronald McDonald shoes.

I put out a hand like a silent apology, as if to say, *oh, man, I'm sorry, are you okay,* but I didn't stop to help him up.

Cash still sat in the highchair, his back to me, my mother-in-law now letting out tiny shrieks. Her mouth was open wide with hands pressed to her cheeks.

I reached him, and removed the tray, lifted him into my arms, and spun around to face my mother-in-law, ready to ask her what the hell her problem was…when I saw Cash's face.

I'd thought he was covered in blue cake frosting. That couldn't be it. The cake was still in the house. We would light candles and sing Happy Birthday after we ate, not before.

Cash's skin was grey, peeling away from the bone. His eyes were not brown and bright, but cloudy and colorless. His white baby teeth looked like something inside the mouth of piranha and snapped as if trying to bite a chunk out of my shoulder.

I dropped him. I dropped my son. He landed on his padded bottom. The diaper absorbed the brunt of the fall. He didn't cry.

He growled.

Cash thrust his hands at me, moaned and latched his tiny arms and hands around my leg. I watched in horror as his mouth opened wide and bit down on my jeans.

I felt a scream struggle its way up my throat before it actually exploded like a siren from my mouth. "No!"

"Dad! Daddy!" Charlene, my fourteen year old daughter, said. I recognized her voice. I could not see her. Where was she?

I thrashed side to side, wanting my son off my leg, his teeth out of my clothing and out of my flesh. "No!"

"Chase, it's a dream. You're having a nightmare." A hand on my shoulder, another rubbed my back.

"Julie?" I said.

The hand fell away. I opened my eyes and looked around. It couldn't have been a dream. Every detail had been so vivid, so real. It wasn't my wife, Julie, who'd awakened me.

"Allison," I said. "Honey, I'm sorry."

Allison was my girlfriend. Julie, she was my *ex-wife*. Calling one the other was never a good idea. The reason and only explanation and possibly only saving grace for why I'd made such a mistake, I'd been asleep. Wasn't on purpose, or even on accident. It was because I actually thought Allison had been her, had been Julie. But Julie was my ex, and she was dead, and I had been the one that killed her.

"What was the nightmare?" Allison said. "Are you okay?"

"I'm okay," I said, but I wasn't. My heart beat fast. I took deep breaths and tried to calm and control my breathing. "I…ah…where are we?"

I'd just asked the question, but I also remembered at that same moment. We were inside a Humvee. It came back to me fast, a flood of memories. My brain fought not to get sucked under as wave after wave of images forced themselves into my mind and crashed around loose and free inside my skull like a mental tsunami.

# # #

At a quick glance, you might think the outbreak came out of nowhere; as if one second, everything was normal and the next zombies were everywhere. The more I think about it, I realize it wasn't how it actually happened. It had been gradual with the signs all there, just no one piecing any of it together. Even if someone had seen what was going on sooner, it wouldn't have changed a thing. It couldn't have.

However, all at once, it came to a head when an overwhelming, overpowering force of walking dead creatures emerged.

Allison and I worked at 911 as dispatchers. That day, I was on phones and took an emergency call from a scientist or a doctor, I can't remember, but he claimed he was partly to blame for the, what would you call it? A problem? An Apocalypse?

The man said that contaminated vials of the swine flu vaccination had been shipped and administered to Americans across the country before the error had been recognized. Inoculated people didn't catch the flu. Instead, they turned into zombies.

Zombie was the only word I could use to describe the completed transformation. Their veins darkened to black and stood out like morbid highlights on pale, pale skin. Eyes lost any vibrancy and color as a milky, cloudy film covered the iris and pupil.

At first, I didn't think a bite could cause another to turn into a zombie. I'd been wrong. Getting bitten by one of those things was bad. Very bad.

Some of the creatures meandered toward you, slow as shit and sluggish. It wasn't a joke. Get surrounded by enough of them, caught off guard, or backed into a corner, and they'd kill you. Eat your flesh and tear into your gut without pause. The others were fast like Kenyans. I'd seen a herd of them chase a man in a mall parking lot, take him down, and rip his flesh to shreds. The threat from either was equal and real.

Allison and I made it out of the 911 facility. I had one goal. I needed to make it across the city and save my kids. Charlene was fourteen, and Cash, who had been nine. By car, we could have made the journey across fifteen miles in twenty minutes, but the streets were littered with abandoned, disabled and crashed vehicles. Forced to trek the distance on foot, twenty minutes became several days. Zombies were everywhere and we had to find shelter often and for long periods of time to keep from getting devoured. It was during this time that we met up with Josh and Dave Rivera.

Josh died. Zombies never touched him. He'd been shot. Someone or some group armed with guns shot at us. They never came out from where they were hidden. They never attacked, but they did manage to kill Josh. Dave had been devastated. I couldn't blame him. His saving grace was Sues Melia. She'd been in a courtyard by a hotel, running from a zombie when we found and saved her. Sues and Dave bonded. They were an odd couple, quiet and reclusive, but it worked for them. Whatever it was, they appeared happy together.

Charlene was a trooper. Tough as nails. I hated clichés, but there was no other way to describe her. She'd taken on some serious responsibility as a fourteen year old, watching out for her brother and she had learned how to use weapons. Not just use them, but used them effectively.

My son, Cash, got caught in the middle of crossfire and took a bullet. Johanna Erway, a paramedic with the Coast Guard, had done all she could to save him. She'd removed the slug, but the damage done internally was worse than we'd imagined. There was bleeding that couldn't be stopped.

Charlene blamed herself. It hadn't been her fault. She was a lot like me, hard headed and hard on herself. Don't think there's anything I could have said, or could say, that would ever change her mind. She was always going to carry the weight of that on her shoulders, as if she felt she was the only one responsible for the death of her little brother.

We were a group of survivors and only a week or so into this mess. We were a small band of people now forced to depend on each other. I often referred to us as a family. We were all we had left: Erway and Elysia Palmeri, a Private from the U.S. Army; Sues Melia, a front desk employee from a hotel; Dave Rivera, someone I consider (an unexpected) close friend; Allison Little, my girlfriend; and my 14 year-old daughter, Charlene, who was *tough as nails*.

That was it. This was my family.

CHAPTER ONE

Monday, November 2nd, 1315 hours

The seven of us were packed into the Humvee we'd confiscated from an internment camp in New York, up north along the St. Lawrence River. I had no idea how long we'd been driving, but I'd managed to fall asleep and have a nightmare about clowns, and my ex, and my dead son, Cash. "Where are we?"

"Not all that far from where we started," Palmeri said. She was in the driver's seat. Erway rode shotgun. "I remember something the Terrigino brothers said while we were with them, might have been at the dinner table."

The Terrigino brothers were survivalists, preppers, hermits living in the woods by Cedar Point Park, where the military had set up a failed internment camp for medical and research purposes. The brothers had invited us into the log cabin they lived in. Place had been stocked with food and weapons. If the Terrignos hadn't been stark raving mad, and the cabin burned to the ground, it would have been an ideal structure to hole up for the winter months.

"What was it they'd said?" Allison asked. She held my hand, had her head turned so she could look toward the front of the vehicle. I stared at her profile. The scraped up little nose, the mud-matted hair, and the scabbing cut across her forehead from an array of reckless car accidents. She was beautiful. I was lucky, and thankful she'd stuck it out with me. I could not be an easy person to love, and much of the time, tougher to even like.

"They mentioned a small airport. Helicopters and planes coming in and out during the weeks prior to the outbreak," Palmeri said.

I remembered them saying as much and thought it suggested guilt on the part of the military.

"What good's an airport? My guess, there aren't going to be pilots on standby, drinking coffee and reading the newspaper," Dave said. "No, I think we just keep driving. Just head south."

"There don't have to be pilots there," Palmeri said.

"Ah, I'm thinking there sure as shit does," Dave said.

Palmeri shrugged. "As long as there is fuel and a plane, I can get us out of here. I know you think Mexico is our best bet, Chase. A plane's going to help us get there a hell of a lot faster than taking roads, and off roads, even in a small tank like this."

I nodded. She was right. "And you can fly? A plane?" I said.

"Have a license and everything," she said, and looked up at me in the reflection of the rearview mirror. "Not on me. You'll just have to take my word."

"Sounds like a plan," I said. "A damn good one."

"Don't go getting all excited yet. A lot is going to depend on what is there and fuel. Fuel is going to play a pretty major role in this plan," she said, smiling. "Let's see if we can find that airport."

Charlene smiled, too.

"What, honey?" I said.

"I was just thinking about the first time we flew together, to Florida."

"Disneyland," I said. "How can you remember? You were a baby."

"Okay," she said. "I don't remember it. I just remember how many times you told the story. Felt like more of a memory, I've heard it so much, like something I actually remembered."

We sat there silent for a moment. Allison nudged me in the side with an elbow.

"Ouch!"

"Are you going to tell us the story?" Allison said.

I looked around. We had, at this point, nothing but time.

"I'll tell it," Charlene said. "Can I, Dad?"

"Yeah, of course." My daughter looked happy and her small smile melted my heart.

"I was maybe nine months old. We flew out of Buffalo on a direct flight to Orlando. My dad had me in his arms getting on the plane, and I was fidgeting and crying a little. He's making his way to our seat and everyone's rolling their eyes at him. Oh yeah, they're thinking, he's that guy. The guy with the baby that's going to cry for four hours," she said, her hands clasped together and rested in her lap. It was the most animated I'd seen her since first finding her and Cash at my apartment in Rochester.

"Hate guys like you," Allison said, and again gave a shot to my gut with her elbow. No way was I admitting those jabs hurt, so I just made a face and playfully pushed her back.

Everyone seemed drawn into the rendition, waiting for Charlene to continue. I even found myself taken in by it, anxious to hear the rest.

Charlene knew what she was doing too, what she was accomplishing. I saw it when we locked eyes for a brief moment. Yes, I knew the memory made her happy, but I also saw the intelligence behind her need to share. The storytelling was a *distraction* that wasn't only helpful, it appeared necessary.

"Dad gets buckled in, my mother next to him. She's digging through the diaper bag for the baggie of Cheerios, teething rings and rattles. She hopes one of those things is going to quiet me down for the flight. Naturally, none of them do. Then the plane is on the tarmac, headed in line for our turn to take off, and before you know it, we start to pick up speed, shooting down the runway. As we lift off the ground, my head just gets lower and lower until it's on my dad's chest, like the force of take-off pushed me against him, and just like that," she said, and snapped her fingers, "I'm asleep and stay asleep for the entire flight."

"No way," Allison said.

"Oh yeah," I said. "The whole flight, and I couldn't move at all. I was afraid if I even tried to open the complimentary bag of peanuts--"

"Found it!" Palmeri said. "Not much of an airport, but I see a helicopter parked next to a hangar."

I hated reality. It seriously knew how to hack the shit out of good times. I gave my daughter a wink. She winked back and lowered her head some, as if suddenly shy.

"Are you licensed to fly a helicopter?" Sues said, pointing at the bird that sat on a pad.

"Ah, no. I'm not."

We seemed to all sigh collectively. "Okay, so now what?" I said.

"We should check the hangar. The size of that thing, fifty-fifty chance a plane is inside," Palmeri said. "Can't hurt to look, anyway."

"Also a fifty-fifty chance the hangar could be filled with mechanic, wrench wielding zombies, too," Dave said. "And pilot zombies. And just, you know, a ton of freaking zombies!"

He was right, of course. "You see any creatures anywhere?" I said.

"No, none," Erway said. "Looks pretty deserted."

"Hate that," Allison said. "Maybe it's just me, but deserted seems a hundred times scarier. At least if we see them, we can handle it. Take them out. But when there is nothing, none of them, I just get that searching the rooms-of-a-haunted-house feeling."

Sues kept nodding her head in agreement.

"Nobody get out of the truck," Erway said, which was a statement that did not need to have been made. "I'm going to check out the hangar. I agree with Allison, not a fan of the deserted. I'm thinking if there are zombies anywhere, they're inside that hangar. So give me a few minutes to see what's what inside."

"I'll go with you," Palmeri said, and unfastened her seatbelt.

"I don't think so," Dave said. "You're our pilot. Kind of a commodity right now. We need you. I'll go with Erway. We'll clear the hangar and signal when it's safe."

I saw Sues' grip tighten on Dave's forearm. Nothing extreme, just her fingers squeezing a bit more than they had been.

This was how it was now. To get from place to place, chances needed to be taken. They would always be dangerous. The unknown was that way. It was never going to seem fair, either. Couldn't be the same people always volunteering. Everyone was going to need to take a chance, a turn. No one wanted to risk their life. I knew I didn't. I knew I was tired. I knew I never wanted to die and leave Charlene all alone. I couldn't imagine a worse fate than that, except her dying.

"Erway is our medic," I said. "She's staying. I'll go with Dave."

"You're talking about me like I'm not here," Erway said.

"No," I said. "That's not what I'm doing. I'm talking to everyone else. Making it clear."

"I can pull my own weight," she said.

"Didn't imply you couldn't. And soon enough, we're going to have to put together a risk-taking rotation." I smiled. "For now, let's not do this. It's not a pissing match. It's like Dave said about Palmeri. A pilot, a medic. That's pretty essential right now. I have a machete. A knife. I can be replaced."

"Stop, Chase," Allison said.

"You know what I mean." I was between Allison and Charlene. I slid forward and knelt in the center of the Humvee. "It's Dave and me. And like Erway said, no one else gets out of this vehicle. No one."

I was referring to my daughter. If anyone was going to risk getting out and coming to help, I envisioned her being the one doing it. I wanted to make sure Allison caught on, and kept Charlene from leaving. I hoped she picked up the meaning by the tone of my voice. I had no way of verifying whether or not she did without coming out and asking, so I decided to play it safer and simply asked, "Am I clear?"

The five of them acknowledged.

"Dave, ready?"

"Ready, sir." He sighed in a long, loud breath. I don't think he meant to let that escape from his lungs in front of everyone. It just sounded like a depressing bag of deflating desperation and surrender.

CHAPTER TWO

Palmeri drove the Humvee up onto the tarmac and stopped by the chopper pad. Dave and I climbed out and walked to the front of the vehicle. I stared at the helicopter. It resembled a prehistoric bird on furlough from a museum. The front of the thing had a *face*. The big windows looked like eyes, the propeller blades draped to either side like eyebrows. I don't know, like I said, to me it looked like a face.

"You okay?" Dave said.

I wasn't sure if I was. When I'd been a kid, we played ding-dong-ditch. One old woman had wind chimes on her front porch. The house was set back from the road. The idea wasn't to ring her doorbell, but to swipe your arm across the chimes. The other kids on the street were older. They forced me to do it. I worked up the courage and made my way up her lawn, staying low, and moving quietly from tree to tree. I could hear the others laughing in the street. They were ready to run and hide as soon as I rang the chimes. When I got up onto the porch, about to run my arm across the wind chimes, a light switched on. That old woman sat in a chair on a corner of the porch waiting. I'd stood frozen, and when she got up to come at me, I found my legs and ran away, screaming at the top of my lungs. I felt that way now, but at least I wasn't alone. "Let's just check this place out."

The clouds were one solid sheet of gunmetal-grey that made up the entire sky for as far as the eye could see. The leafless trees stood like skeletons along most of the perimeter. The wind had picked up, brisk and bone-chilling. It smelled wet, as if rain or snow was in the inevitable future. The crisp air filled and stung my lungs. It was going to be a long, harsh winter for survivors in the north. Hibernating the next several months would prove challenging. I prayed they found shelter safe from zombies and full of supplies. None of that seemed likely, though.

Before fleeing the burning cabin, most of us had escaped with weapons from the Terrigino stash. Stocking up on rifles and ammo, machetes, swords and knives, I wore a machete and sheath on my back and a long sword with a scabbard and nine-inch sawbuck-hunting knife on my hip, completely foregoing a rifle or sidearm. I learned the hard way how frightening it was to be surrounded by zombies and out of ammunition. My daughter dressed similarly. Dave had a rifle and a sidearm. Between the two of us, I figured that even if we ran into a flock of zombies, we'd be able to deliver some serious damage before being forced to retreat. I hoped, anyway, because in every instance, it seemed like retreat was inexorable.

The Humvee's engine let out a low and steady chugging sound; it was just a bit less than a grumble, and a tad more than a purr. Other than that, the only thing making noise was the wind. It sounded angry, if you wanted to personify it, and ran along the hangar rattling the loose aluminum walls, rocked the helicopter's blades and caused me to shiver against its force. I wished the vest I wore was equipped with both sleeves and a collar, but then it wouldn't be a vest. In truth, the shiver might only be partly caused by the frigid air.

The hangar resembled a giant warehouse with a bowed roof, and appeared secured. The doors that let planes in and out were rolled closed. There was a normal door as well. I motioned to Dave with my head that we'd start that way. "Only real door I see," I said. "Let's check it out."

With a slight nod, Dave followed me.

I held the machete by my side and gripped the handle, wishing I'd taken a pair of thin gloves from the Terrignos. Continued use of this thing was going to rub my palms raw. While the rubber might be better to hold than wood, sweat and blood would still make it slippery and difficult to hold, I'd bet.

We reached the hangar, and stood on either side of the front entrance. I put a wrist to my chest, feeling my heartbeat through my clothing.

"Could be a back door, too," Dave said.

"Probably is," I said. "Should we do a walk-around?"

Dave shook his head. "If there's a door, there's a door. If there isn't…" He shrugged. His way of saying, *Oh well*, without saying it.

"I'm good with that," I said. I switched the machete to my other hand and tried the doorknob. Twisted it left and right. Barely moved. "Locked."

"Of course. We kick it in, or whatever. If there aren't any zombies around, they'll start this way. If there are zombies inside, it'll be like ringing the doorbell," Dave said. "I hate this shit."

"Hating it right along with you," I said. Don't know how many times I cursed at home about having to go into work. The idea of being tethered by a headset to a workstation for eight plus hours gave me stomach cramps. Then there was that, stomach cramps. You basically had to raise your hand and get permission from a supervisor to use the bathroom. Right now, though, with things the way they were, I'd take being treated like a fucking preschooler over this any day of the week. "You see any other option?"

"We take that walk-around, see if there is another door, and check if that one is unlocked," Dave said. "Unless you want to just kick this one in?"

I looked back at the Humvee. It was parked maybe fifty yards away. Couldn't see through the front windshield since the glass was heavily tinted. I knew everyone inside was staring directly at us. They were counting on us. "Let's walk it. Make it quick. There has got to be an easy way inside."

We made our way along the west side of the hangar. I've never been in the jungle before, not the Serengeti, Congo, or the Amazon, and yet, I knew Dave and I were being followed. I couldn't help feel like a gazelle. Out there was a lion, or a pack of lions. I knew it. I held up a fist.

We stopped.

"What?" Dave said, it was a whisper.

"We're being followed."

We both spun around.

I laughed first, Dave a millisecond later. I'd been correct. We were being followed. A giant black Humvee had closed the sixty yard gap between us. It was ten yards away, and inching closer and closer. "Guess we're all going for that walk around the hangar," I said.

"Nothing wrong with that," Dave said. "Not a thing."

I agreed. While there was safety in numbers, having a vehicle filled with armed people on your side only helped. Didn't hurt.

Once at the corner of the building, I peeked around the side, quickly.

"Well? Is it clear?" Dave said.

I placed my back against the building. My cheeks felt numb. The temperature had to be dropping fast. My breath came out in plumes.

I shook my head, and let out a little laugh. "I looked too fast. I didn't see anything."

"You okay?" Dave said.

I nodded. "Ah-yeah, peachy."

Dave stuck his head around the corner. "It's clear."

"Awesome," I said. "Sorry about that."

"Nothing to be sorry for," he said.

But there was something to be sorry for. I felt unraveled. The coming undone took place inside of me, in my head, and chest. Those parts of me seemed like fabric tearing away, being peeled back. I'd lost my son yesterday, and buried him this morning. There had been no time to stop, grieve, mourn, or to heal. None. Nothing.

Dave knew what it felt like, what I was going through. He'd lost his brother only days before that.

Over the last week, all of us had lost someone. Every one of us. I just needed a way to keep pushing on, moving forward, even though I didn't want to. That was honest and raw. It was the way I felt. I didn't want to try anymore. I wasn't sure there was a point. Other than caring for Allison and Charlene, I was drained. They might be the only two reasons I didn't just give up altogether. Just lay down my weapons, curl into a ball and just fall asleep forever.

The plan to go to Mexico was flat and uninspired. I had everyone all rallied and excited about crossing the foreign border. The fucking zombies were everywhere. The disease would only continue to spread. Things would get worse before they ever got even slightly better. However, things getting any worse was nearly incomprehensible. If Mexico was in any better shape than New York, I'd be more than surprised, I'd be shocked. Fucking shocked.

"Chase," Dave said. His voice worked at pulling me out of my internal mental melee and back into our reality.

"I'm ready. I'm good. I'll go first," I said.

I didn't need to go around that corner first, though. The Humvee pulled ahead. They must have realized we were looking for another way into the hangar, and were making sure the back of the building had clear access, should there be a second door.

The Humvee stopped behind the building.

Dave and I rounded the corner. "A door," he said.

"It better not be locked." We stayed close to the building.

"Smell that?" Dave said. He looked back over his shoulder toward the east. "Fire somewhere."

"I do. Guessing a lot of the country is burning right about now," I said. "The dry leaves piled up everywhere --people in homes with no furnace starting small fires indoors to keep warm. There are going to be a lot of fires." A lot of deaths. Smoke, and CO poisoning. We stood at the door. "You gonna try it?"

Dave wrapped his hands on the knob and twisted. We both heard the soft release-click. Unlocked. He looked at me. I nodded, signaling he should pull it open when he was ready.

He silently mouthed, *One, two, three.*

I stood in front of the doorway, machete in a two-handed grip, the blade pointed at the asphalt.

The door stood open.

It was so windy out that it was difficult to hear if there was any movement inside the hangar. There could be a party inside, and I wasn't hearing it. "I'm going in," I said.

"I'm right behind you."

I stepped inside slowly, cautiously, looking left and right. There were no windows, not even on the doors. It was great to get out of the wind. Once inside, the noise from that wind subsided some. I listened hard for any sound of movement. It was too dark to see much of anything, and somehow, the room still felt large and foreboding. It reminded me of the time Allison and I drove through West Virginia on our way to Georgia. It had been the middle of the night and the road was full of twisted turns and curves and tunnels. You couldn't see anything except what lay dead-ahead in the shallow beam of the car's headlights. The Allegheny Mountains hugged every stretch of road, and despite a splash of light now and then from vehicles headed in the opposite direction, it was a pitch black that consumed everything and yet, you just sensed the size and greatness of the mountain range. They were a clear and obvious presence, both inducing a level of fear and comfort, perhaps because they have stood for centuries hidden at night by the nothingness of darkness.

I stepped to the left, backed up against the wall and felt around for a light switch. "Check along the wall by you for a light," I said.

Somewhere, something fell over and rolled. The noise echoed and was loud enough that I jumped and banged my shoulder into the wall. It sounded hollow, like an empty paint can, or some kind of tin bucket. "Dave?" I said, and hoped he'd knocked something over.

"Wasn't me. Guessing it wasn't you, then?"

"No, not me. Shit." It's what I feared. My hand ran up and down the wall with a bit more urgency. There had to be a switch. Rooms all over the world kept light switches on the wall by a door. It was common fucking sense, to be expected. And yet, I couldn't find a switch.

Lights came on, slowly, the long fluorescents buzzed and flickered, running along the walls and then finally lit the whole place with blinding brilliance.

I saw it and with no time to kill, dropped to the ground and rolled out of the way. The zombie was fast and lunged at me. Before I could get back up onto my feet, it was on me, knocked the machete from my hands and out of reach. It growled and grunted as it pinned me down.

Most of the thing's lower lip was gone. The flesh peeled away and hung from the bottom of his chin. A steady flow of thick, slow oozing black blood drooled from the corners of its severed mouth. Patches of the thing's hair were chunked away from its skull. One swollen eye was shut, the lid looked blistered as if severely burned. The days of zombie life had not been kind to this creature. If I got my way, things would get a lot worse.

At this angle, though, with me on my back and the freaking thing straddling me, I could not reach the machete. Only thing I could do was unclip the sheath on my hip and pull the hunting knife free. I shouted over and over, "Dave!"

I heard a struggle coming from somewhere else in the room. Sound echoed and carried and bounced around and against the walls like a fucking whacked out racquetball.

I took hold of the zombie's shirt collar and pulled him down toward me. As I brought my other arm up fast, I punched the blade into the thing's ear. Something popped and before it fell off me, an eyeball rolled free from the left socket.

I managed to get onto my knees and stand up. I gasped, a hand over my stomach and bent forward. There was no time to catch my breath. Dave was pinned on the floor and using a forearm to keep from being bitten. I scraped up the machete as I ran toward them. I took a final step closer and swung the blade around. Wasn't looking to just make it to first base with that swing. I wanted a home run and aimed for the fences. The zombie's head did not launch toward the hangar's ceiling the way I'd envisioned, but fell away from the shoulders and bounced twice before it skidded to a stop on the cement flooring.

Dave pushed the remaining torso to the side. More of that thick, black blood oozed from this zombie's neck and slowly drained from the corpse the way maple syrup pours onto pancakes. "Fuck! He smells," Dave said. "These things seem like they're rotting away."

I kicked the corpse, the finally dead corpse, and offered a hand to Dave. "At least it was worth it," I said.

"Worth it, how," he said.

"Look," I said.

Behind me was a twin engine plane. It filled a good portion of the front of the hangar.

"How do we fuel one of these things up?"

I shook my head. "I guess we need Palmeri now."

As I walked toward the door we'd just entered, the Humvee horn blared.

I looked back at Dave.

His eyes were open wide. Horn could only mean one thing…

CHAPTER THREE

The Humvee's horn screamed like a bass siren. Palmeri wasn't just honking it, she was laying on it.

I ran for the door, reached it in four steps and shielded my eyes from the Humvee headlights. The passenger door on the Humvee flew open. "Get back in the truck! Come on, get in!" Erway waved at Dave and me with frantic hand gestures.

"Dave!" I said.

"I hear it," he said. "Zombies?"

"Gotta be!" We exited the hangar. I couldn't see what caused the excitement.

"The plane," Dave said. He pointed back from where we'd come out of, and waved it away, as if saying, *ah forgiddaboudit.*

I climbed into the Humvee. "There's a plane inside."

"Zombies coming this way," Charlene said. She was looking out the side window after Dave got in and shut the door. "I mean, a lot of zombies are coming right at us."

As soon as Dave was inside and the door closed, Palmeri gave the vehicle gas. Tires protested on pavement as she cut the wheel one way, then the other to get around the hangar. "They came out of nowhere!"

Then I saw them.

They must have come from the woods. They ran at us. Crazed looking. Some wore military clothing. Others were in flannel and hunting camo. Others were flat out naked, or wearing such torn and tattered clothing that nothing was identifiable.

"Holy shit," Dave said.

"Now what? We don't want to just leave the plane," I said.

"We don't even know if it's fueled, or if it's a plane I can fly," Palmeri said.

"It had two propellers. One on each wing. Is that something you can fly?" Dave said.

"It could be," Palmeri said. She drove back toward the way we'd initially come.

"I left the door open to the hangar," Dave said.

"Forget about it," I said, and almost laughed.

"What?" Dave said.

I shook my head. "Nothing."

"How many do you count?" Erway said. "I see, I'd say, twenty."

"It's what I see," Charlene said.

"We're not getting out of this Humvee," I said. Not a chance. "They're fast, every one of them."

"While your machete looks really cool," Erway said, and held up her AK47, "this is better equipped to handle a situation like this. We need that airplane. I have no idea if Mexico is the answer, but New York is shot to shit. Palmeri, circle back around."

Palmeri pursed her lips, but turned the wheel.

"Stop close, but not too close," Erway said.

Once the Humvee came to a complete stop, Erway aimed the AK out the window. "Going to be a little loud, folks," she said, before squeezing the trigger.

I took Allison's hand.

Not every shot was a headshot. She dropped three quickly. Blood, brains and skull exploding onto the other walkers. Two, she hit in the gut. Bullets ripped away slabs of flab. It slowed them some, but didn't stop them. Erway paused and took a deep breath. She exhaled and went back to work.

The sound inside the Humvee was deafening. Allison kept her eyes closed, shoulders hunched. She twitched as shots were fired. Charlene and I locked eyes.

The remaining zombies closed the gap, getting closer and closer to the Humvee. I watched Palmeri. She kept both hands on the steering wheel, ready to punch the gas pedal with both feet if those things got too close.

The final few, she took more time. Aimed. Dropped them one after the other. The last zombie was, at best, twenty feet away from the vehicle. Looked like the bullet pummeled the thing in the left eye socket. It took several stumbling steps forward before another round exploded through its forehead.

Erway smiled, sat back, butt of the AK on the Humvee car mat. "I cannot lie. I kind of enjoyed that."

I didn't smile and could not see how cutting down even twenty zombies would be enjoyable. These were people at one time, still were, actually. My stomach churned some.

Allison shook her head, staring at me.

"We going back for the plane?" Charlene said.

"I think we should. All that gunfire is bound to attract more of them to the area. We either try to get out of here in the air, or I say we hit the road and just start heading south," Dave said.

"I agree," Sues said.

"Ok," Palmeri said. "We're going back."

"You can do this?" Allison said. She leaned up front between the set of seats. "Fly a plane? I mean, you've got a license, I know. You said that, but fly a plane, a big military plane?"

I touched Allison on the back. Her fear of flying was borderline psychotic. Many people did not like flying, but flew. Allison flew once with her family when she was young. They were going on a family vacation to California. The flight was choppy at best, as if pockets of turbulence aligned specifically for the plane she and her family were in. Her mother had a hell of a time getting her to fly back home when the trip came to an end. There were bribery attempts and promises made, but it came down to flat out threats and damning punishments that finally convinced her to get on the flight home. That had been seven days later, so there was a good chance they'd have better weather on that flight. Only Allison was not so lucky. The turbulence was worse. The landing gear wouldn't lower. Fire trucks and ambulances were on standby at the end of the runway when they landed. Allison didn't just fear flying, she hated it.

"We'll know, once we get in the hangar," Palmeri said. That hadn't exactly been a reassuring statement, however, it had been honest. "If I can't fly it, I won't. No sense getting something up in the air just because I can, if I am not completely confident I can bring her back down safely."

I wanted to clap a hand against my forehead. Did she really just say that?

Allison sat back, her eyes filled with terror. Her lips quivered and her body trembled. I don't think she could've spoken a word if she wanted. I pulled her into my arms, hugged her tight. Charlene just looked at me with a look I knew all too well. I arched my eyebrows, hopefully telling my daughter to show some compassion. Instead, Charlene rolled her eyes and turned away.

The Humvee stopped by the hangar's back door. We sat inside because it seemed like no one wanted to move just yet.

Palmeri shut the engine, put the keys in her breast pocket. "On three, we make a run for the hangar."

"A run?" Sues said. "I don't see any more zombies."

"That don't mean it's time to walk," Erway said.

"I don't think I can do this," Allison said.

"What's wrong?" Dave said.

"Nothing," I said.

"Chase." Allison fisted my shirt as she lifted her head off my chest. "We should drive to Mexico. We should."

"Why do you want to drive?" Sues said.

"She's afraid to fly." Charlene crossed her arms. "Dad, we don't have time for this."

My daughter was right. We didn't have time for this. "Honey, more zombies will be coming. They heard the gunshots. They are going to come from every direction. We're kind of committed--"

"To flying? No we're not." Allison narrowed her eyes at me, wanting me to know there was still room to debate.

There wasn't. "This flight will not be like the other two you were on."

"You don't know that. What did you say? You said this plane, the one in there, has two propellers? Propellers, Chase? I was on a plane with engines. Jet engines. The one in that hangar has propellers, and you think a flight to Mexico with a pilot who happens to have a license is going to be smoother than JetBlue? No offense, Elysia."

"None taken," she said.

"We're going to check out the plane," I said.

"I'll wait here while you check. Elysia, may I have the keys?" Allison held out her hand.

"Dad?" Charlene raised her eyebrow at me, this time. She wasn't asking me to be compassionate though.

"We're all going into the hangar, Alley. I am not leaving you out here."

"We're going on three." Erway put her hand on the door handle.

"Wait, wait, wait!" Allison grabbed onto my arm. "This isn't a good idea. Flying to Mexico. It's not a good idea. We should drive."

"You said that, already." Charlene placed a hand on Allison's shoulder. "We have to go. You can do this. You can hold my hand the entire time. I won't let go, not once, but we need to move. We need to keep moving and we need to stay together. We're not going to leave you alone in this truck, and I'm not going to let go of your hand on that plane."

Allison loosened her grip on my shirt. "Thank you."

They hugged.

"This is great, but we really, really need to get inside that hangar." Erway pushed open her door.

CHAPTER FOUR

1540 hours

We stood inside the hangar with the doors closed and the Humvee parked just outside the back door in case the plane option didn't pan out. Staring at the size of the plane, I couldn't help feeling a bit apprehensive. It was fat, bulky. Despite propellers on each wing, I didn't think this thing was ever built to fly. *Aerodynamically challenged* is what I would have labeled it.

"Zombie!" Charlene raised her machete, pointing the tip of the blade behind us.

Dave had left the hangar doors open when we escaped earlier. Something must have gotten in.

Erway aimed her AK 47.

"No!" Palmeri held up her hand. "You can't fire a gun in here. There might be fuel around."

The zombie was by a red toolbox on wheels. It held a wrench in one hand. It didn't look so much like a weapon as it did a tool, like the thing wanted to get back to work and make repairs on the plane.

What repairs did the plane need?

Then the mechanic-zombie charged. I raised my machete and used a sweep of my arm to push Charlene behind me before taking several steps forward. It came at me fast. I held the handle with two hands and let out a roar as I chopped at its head.

The blade buried itself more than an inch into the thing's

forehead and face, parting the bridge of its nose nearly in half. Its eyes rolled upward, as a thick black tongue protruded from the corner torn flesh of its mouth.

"Check around, and make sure this was the only one," I said. The hangar didn't have rooms. It was basically big, and empty, except for the large plane.

"Clear," Charlene said, she held onto her machete with two hands. "I don't see anymore."

We encircled Palmeri, then, and waited.

"Well?" Sues said, finally. "Is it something you can fly?"

Palmeri nodded and walked from the back of the plane around to the front, and back again. The rest of us stood still, silent, and continued waiting.

"I've not flown one of *these*." Palmeri pointed at the plane. "However, I have flown twin propeller planes before. Just not one like this, this…big."

"So we're driving?" Allison held onto Charlene's hand. I saw how white their knuckles were. Alley must have been squeezing the hell out of my daughter.

"This is a cargo plane, but it can seat up to thirty people." Palmeri moved a four-step ladder close to the door on the side of the plane. "With a full tank of gas, she'll take us, three, three hundred and fifty miles?"

"Mexico is a lot further than that," Sues said.

"It's a three hundred mile head start. Will put us somewhere in, I don't know exactly, like southern New York, or Pennsylvania?" Dave said. "How long will a flight like that take?"

"We should hit Pennsylvania for sure. And In this? It'll take roughly a few hours. Figure we can cruise a little over two hundred miles an hour. Thing is, the plane's not pressurized." Palmeri climbed the steps and opened the side door.

"What's that? I mean, what's that mean?" Allison shook her head, let go of my daughter and walked toward the steps.

"It means the back door on this baby doesn't seal right. Going to be a little loud and a little cold back there. Wasn't exactly built for luxury. It's a nice plane, though. Solid. It's about fifty-eight feet long, with a seventy-four foot wingspan." Palmeri sounded like she might be talking to herself, going over what she knew, and what she thought she might need to know to about flying this plane. She disappeared inside the plane.

"Chase, I don't like this. Any of it. She doesn't know how to fly this. She admitted it. She said she'd never flown a plane this big. What did she tell me in the truck, huh? She said if she couldn't fly it, she wouldn't. Sounds to me like she can't fly it, so we shouldn't risk it."

"Give her a minute," I said. "Let her look around, take a peek at the controls. If she sounds hesitant, we'll drive."

"We will? You promise? Because right now, I look like the crazy one."

"You don't look crazy. You look scared. It's okay to be scared."

"Promise me. Just say it. Say you promise we'll drive if she doesn't sound like she knows what she's doing."

"I promise."

Charlene grunted and walked away.

Erway appeared impatient. She held onto her AK and walked around the plane. "I don't think we can start this thing up in here."

"We can't." Palmeri was at the doorway. "See that buggy? Once we open the hangar doors, it will pull us out of the hangar toward the runway. Once outside, we can fire up the engines."

"Propellers," Allison said.

"Can you fly it?" Sues said.

"I can. I'm going to need someone up front with me, assisting with the controls. It's a two-pilot job," she said.

Allison stared at me. I couldn't say anything. Palmeri sounded confident.

"Shotgun," Erway said.

Palmeri came down the stairs. She took a thick braided rope with a hook from the back of the buggy and hooked it onto the front of the plane. "Going to need to open the hangar doors and for someone to drive this thing."

We all needed to take turns. It was the one thing that kept coming around. Just like there were a million things to volunteer for before now, there will be this instance, and then a million more after. Each time the threat of danger and dying would be possible, if not probable and prevalent.

"I've got it," Sues said, and raised her hand like she was about to answer a question.

Dave grabbed her arm. She shrugged out of his hold. "Sues," he said.

"I can't sit anymore," she said. "I can't just be on the sidelines. We're a family. Chase said so more than once. And we need to take turns doing these crazy things. We need to. This, driving that buggy and pulling this plane out of the hangar, this is my crazy thing I get to do. You need to let me, Dave. I need to do this."

Palmeri pointed. "Dave, Chase, move those blocks set in front of and behind the wheels. Everyone else, get on the plane."

"She'll be okay," I said to Dave.

"I don't like this." He sounded like Allison. "I'm opening the hangar door. She can pull the plane out, but I'm not getting on until she does."

"I'm not arguing. That's what you should do. It's what I'd do." I smiled.

"You would?"

"Yes. If it were Allison, it's what I'd do. Same thing."

"Okay. Good. Go get on the plane. We got this," Dave said.

I moved the rolling steps out of the way, kicked it toward the hangar wall and hoisted myself up and into the plane.

"Where's Dave?" Allison stood next to my daughter. They were still hand holding.

I'd never been inside a plane like this. Saw them in movies. To my right were roughly twenty fold-down seats, ten on each side of the fuselage. "Is this where we sit?"

"Did you see them?" Allison pointed. "Those don't look safe to sit in at a picnic, much less going three hundred miles an hour thirty-thousand feet in the sky."

"I think she said we'll go around two hundred miles an hour," my daughter said.

"Char," I said.

"Sorry."

"Why don't you two go get buckled in," I said.

"Wait. Dave. Where's Dave?" Allison said.

"He's going to open the hangar door for Sues," I said. "Go

buckle in."

On the left was the door to the cockpit. I opened it. There was room to walk in, but then the pilot and co-pilot needed to climb up and over the center console to slide into their seats. Erway and Palmeri were packed in tight.

"We set in back," Erway said.

"Seems like it." I stared out the front window. Dave was just about to pull open the hangar doors. Palmeri had maps unfolded in front of her. "What are you working on?"

"Flight plan. GPS is down. Would have been able to plug in to in an airport, or something. Doing it old school. Charting our course. Good thing is, I don't expect too much company in the sky. Think we're going to have it pretty much to ourselves," Palmeri said.

The hangar door was open all the way, and now Dave ran the hook from the back of the buggy toward the front of the plane. I lost sight of him.

The plane rocked forward. I held onto the cockpit walls for balance, to keep from falling backward. "We're really doing this?"

"We are." Palmeri held the W-shaped control wheel between her thighs, a hand on each grip.

We were slowly wheeled out of the hangar. Sues led us cautiously toward the runway. "That enough runway to get us out of here?"

"Has to be. They landed this thing here, right?" Palmeri said.

I shook my head. "Really doesn't look long enough."

Palmeri didn't say a word. Possibly she agreed, and if she did so out loud, knew it would make everyone that much more apprehensive about flying.

Sues stopped the buggy, turned with one arm draped over the seat and stared at the plane. Without being able to see what was happening, I'd guess Dave was running to unhook the rope from the front.

"Go get your seat. Buckle in. It's going to be bumpy, loud and cold."

"Yeah, I get that," I said, and turned to leave but stopped. "Will there be any movie, or meal served? I didn't see a single stewardess--"

"Ask a flight attendant," Erway said. "We're pilots."

"Right," I said, and smiled, knowing the slight attempt at humor was appreciated. "Well, there were no flight attendants anywhere--"

Palmeri yelled. "Ah, shit! They need help!"

I looked out the window again. I couldn't see what caused alarm, but neither was I going to wait to find out. I ran out of the cockpit.

"What is it?" Allison said.

"Stay!" I said.

I went out the opened door on the side of the plane and jumped the few feet down to the tarmac. "Dave!"

The buggy was off to the side, a chopped up zombie on the ground beside it. Dave held Sues in his arms. "She's not dead! She's okay. She's going to be fine, Chase. She's all right."

CHAPTER FIVE

Sues Melia was far from fine. Dave was wrong. Her eyes were open, and she was breathing. The zombie bit her shoulder. Shredded cloth and skin flapped in the November breeze. Holding her tight, Dave kept telling me how everything was going to be okay.

"Let's get her on the plane," I said. It was against better judgment. Taking a now-infected person onto the plane with us would be foolish, but more than foolish, dangerous. Dave had my back since the start of this thing. I'd watched him bury his brother. I couldn't tell him to just leave her. Should have, but couldn't.

"Help me, Chase. Help me." Dave reminded me of a child. His tears streaked the dirt from his face. His hands covered in blood kept shifting their hold on Sues' body.

I knelt beside them. "How are you feeling, Sues?"

"I don't want to turn into one of them." It was a mere whisper. I heard it, though.

"We're going to help you," I said.

The lie was just as bold as it was obvious. Might be the only one who believed it was Dave. The smile he wore was forming on trembling lips. "That's, right, honey. We're going to help you. We are. I am."

I looked back at the plane. I knew Erway and Palmeri had to be watching. I couldn't see into the cockpit, but I felt their eyes on me. I could almost feel their thoughts. Feel them. *What's the hold up? Come on. We have to go.*

"Let's carry her to the plane," I said, and stood up.

32

"I'm not going with you, Chase. I'm not going anywhere." The color in her face drained before my eyes. Her skin clammy, lips grey almost blue.

"She's lost a lot of blood," I said.

"We need to stop the bleeding," Dave said.

Stop the bleeding, I thought. What good would it do? "Let's just get her to the plane. Erway can have a closer look."

Sues grabbed my shirt tight and I was surprised by the strength exhibited when she pulled me close. "I'm not going. You need to take care of Dave. You need to be there for him. He looks up to you. You know that, don't you? That he looks up to you?"

"Stop it, honey. We're going to get you on that plane. Tell her, Chase, Tell her Erway can help her. We can stop this. Fix it. You, you're not going to be like one of them. You won't turn into one of those things," he said. That smile he'd worn was gone. He ran his hands through his hair, brushing in dirt and sweat, and Sues' blood. "Chase, man. Chase."

"Sues," I said, "let us get you to the plane, okay? We'll sort this out on the plane. We need to get off the tarmac. No telling how many more of those things are coming this way. And like this--" I looked around, "--we're sitting ducks. You know? We're out in the open."

"Let's just get you onto the plane," Dave said.

"Shoot me," Sues said. "Get it over with. Just end this for me."

I got under an arm, and lifted Sues up off of Dave. He got under the other, and we hoisted her up onto her feet. "That hurts," she said, and winced.

"We're almost to the plane," Dave said. We weren't. We shuffled forward, Sues' feet nearly toe-dragging on the asphalt.

Allison stood in the doorway at the top of the small set of stairs. "Is she okay?"

"Gonna be fine," Dave said.

I kept my eyes on Allison's. She knew better. No one needed to be a zombie apocalyptic expert these days to recognize bad when bad was thrust into your face. And for Sues, this was bad.

Only thing was, it wasn't Sues I was worried about. A bullet to the head, it didn't sound like such a bad thing. We were struggling to survive, and I had my daughter to think of, but for what? Why were we doing this? Why were on the go, always moving, trying to get from here to anywhere else? There was no reason. The human race might be just about over, quickly becoming extinct. It could happen. Something wiped out the fucking dinosaurs. Doubt it was a zombie pandemic, but it was something. Their time to rule ended. People came next. Once we were destroyed, you couldn't help but wonder what would be the next King of the Shit species.

Allison came down the steps. She took Dave's spot. "Go fix her a spot in back," she said. "We got her."

Dave ran up the steps and disappeared into the plane.

"This is wrong," Sues said. "Please, with him gone, kill me."

"We're not killing you," Allison said.

Not yet, I thought. The thing was, the time would come. What if it happened in the air and she turned on the plane?

"You can't let this happen," Sues said. She felt frail and weak. Allison and I supported all of her weight. "You can't put everyone else in danger. I saw what happened to that guy on the boat, on the Coast Guard vessel. He'd been bitten, and tried to hide it, but it caught up to him. When he turned, that was the most horrible thing I'd ever seen."

I couldn't tell her it wasn't going to happen to her. She knew it was going to happen. She knew she was on borrowed time, especially with how much blood she'd lost. And I remembered it, too. Nick Dentino. He'd been with two other civilian survivors rescued by Palmeri and the military. They'd all watched him go from human to fucking zombie right before their eyes. Then they shot him. They could have shot him first, saved him the agony and the suffering, maybe even the humiliation of the transformation. Instead, we'd all watched. Waited and watched. When it was complete, the military shot him.

The plane's engine started, and I nearly jumped back. I didn't expect it to whine so loudly. It startled me. I almost needed my hands to cover my ears. The twin propellers spun slowly, gained momentum and then were twirled so fast I couldn't see the spinning blades.

The decision to kill Sues before getting on the plane was past.

Dave was back at the doorway. "Hurry. We've got zombies coming out of the woods. The sound of the engine must be drawing them."

Allison and Dave got Sues up the stairs and into the plane. I climbed into the plane, and then on my belly, reached down and brought the rolling stairs into the plane with us before closing and locking the door.

We were as safe as we could be in the plane. "Everyone buckle in," I said.

Allison helped Dave get Sues situated. They sat her in a seat toward the tail of the plane. At least she was away from my daughter. I hated to think that way, but I was a parent. What other way could I look at it?

I made the motion of pulling the seat belt tight. Charlene gave me a thumbs up. I smiled, and returned the gesture. I stuck my head into the cockpit. "Tell me you can do this, Palmeri?"

"I can do this," she said. "We've mapped out some airports and coordinates. No GPS, so kind of flying blind. Got an idea of a best-route. Like I said, we should make it to the western part of Pennsylvania. Won't make it even halfway to Texas, but we'll be a few hundred miles closer."

"Okay, okay, that's good," I said.

"Now go get strapped in. Take-offs are hard as shit!"

She didn't laugh. I wish she had. Then I could have convinced myself she was just kidding.

"What's the deal with Sues?" Erway had a paper map unfolded on her lap. There was a math protractor and some pencils on the console between the pilot chairs.

"Bit," I said. "Bad."

"Come here," Palmeri said. She kept her hands on the controls. They both wore headphones, with radios wired to each other so that if nothing else, they could talk easily to each other.

I got as close as I could. I couldn't help staring at all the dials and knobs and switches. They weren't just in front of the pilots. They were above them as well. They were everywhere. There were so many gauges, I wondered how much help Erway could be, having never been a co-pilot before.

"The plane is not pressurized," Palemri said, and then nodded,

35

like that made sense to me.

"You told us. It's going to be cold. Thought I saw a tarp or two back there. We'll use them as blankets. I think we'll manage the cold for a few hours."

"In a regular plane, you know Delta or something, you fire a gun in a pressurized plane you risk killing everyone on board. A gunshot can really fuck things up. Back there, you can fire a shot or two and as long as you don't shoot fuel tanks or some shit like that, it isn't going to mess much up. You see what I'm saying there?"

I saw what she was saying. If Sues became a threat. I could shoot her.

CHAPTER SIX

1702 hours

Allison sat next to Charlene. They were buckled in. I looked at Dave. He wasn't looking at me. He was seated next to Sues, holding her hand. He was talking to her. Whispering. I couldn't hear a single word, but could imagine what was said. He was soothing her, telling her over and over that things would work out, and that she wouldn't turn into a zombie.

I joined my daughter and girlfriend. They saved me the seat between them. I buckled in, and placed a hand on Charlene's leg. "You okay, honey?"

She nodded.

I stared across the narrow aisle. Couldn't take my eyes off Dave and Sues. Her eyes were closed. From where I was it didn't seem like she was breathing. The blood seemed to have stopped flowing from the bite on her shoulder. The raw meat that was exposed looked wet, gooey.

"I think she's dying," Allison said.

I hoped Dave couldn't hear her. The engines were loud, but when something was loud, people tended to whisper that much louder.

Before I could respond, the plane rolled forward. Allison grabbed my hand, my whole arm, actually. "I don't like this. I'm not going to like this."

"We'll be fine," I said, and wondered how different was my

statement from the one Dave kept promising Sues. Would we be fine, or was Palmeri going to crash us from a ten thousand feet?

The plane picked up speed. The whining got louder and louder. There were no windows back here. We couldn't see outside of the plane at all. That might be a good thing. We wouldn't see the zombies lining the runway. We wouldn't see the end of the tarmac as the plane accelerated. We wouldn't see the treetops or mountains or road, or river should we crash into them.

Time moved at an irrationally slow speed. The runway had not seemed long at all, and yet, we were still on it, going faster and faster. If we didn't lift off the ground soon, we'd surely run out of asphalt. How fast did we need to be going before flight was possible? Were all planes different? This box of a plane didn't seem aerodynamic at all. Maybe I'd said that already. My fear wasn't much different from Allison's in this particular situation. Give me JetBlue any day. But a military person with a private license did absolutely nothing to ease my…uneasiness.

The plane left the runway and the nose angle upward. We were up and flying, rising into the sky. I closed my eyes and tried to picture it. I wanted to be up front in the cockpit. I did not like not having control of the situation. Our souls were in Palmeri's hands. Despite the steady drone from the engines, I heard a "woot, woot" from the cockpit.

Would she risk all of our lives if she didn't feel somewhat confident that she could do this? Did we really have any other choice?

We did. We had another choice. We'd left a pretty safe Humvee by the hangar. We could have taken roads and back roads and driven through New York, and Pennsylvania and made our way west, toward the Mississippi, across it and eventually further south to Texas, and eventually reached the Mexican border. The walls I felt sure would protect non-infected humans from the spreading virus that plagued our country, and other countries as well.

The plane tilted to the left, a hard turn in the sky. There were no ground control or radio towers to assist with navigation. Erway used the maps that must have been in compartments or drawers. They were all Palmeri had to rely on to get us as far south-west as we could go before this thing used up the last of its fuel.

"How are you doing?" I said.

Allison tried to smile. She squeezed my hand harder than Julie had during child labor. "I just want to get this flight out of the way."

"Close your eyes," I said. "Try to sleep."

She grunted.

I looked at my daughter. "You okay?"

"Not at all," she said.

I pursed my lips into a thin smile. It was an honest answer. Raw and open and honest. If she'd said she was fine, she'd of been lying. I leaned forward and kissed the top of her head.

She rested it against my chest as best she could, straining slightly against the seatbelts restraints.

# # #

I had arrived to work early, was having coffee in the break room with Allison. A few other people were in there as well. Outside, a blizzard raged. The snow accumulated several inches an hour for the last seven hours. Snow plows and salt trucks couldn't keep up and were running out of places to push the snow.

The supervisor, Milzy, came off the work floor and into the break room. "Guys want some overtime?"

I looked at Allison. She shrugged. She held up her coffee, a way of saying no.

"Sure," I said.

"Grab a phone," he said. "We're like twenty calls in queue."

I'm not exactly sure what people thought. When it was busy, there were only so many telecommunicators to answer calls. Once all lines were tied up, callers waited for the next available person to answer. There were not countless people sitting around waiting to answer ringing phones. So pissed off people often contacted reporters for interviews to express their dissatisfaction with the city. Wouldn't change anything. Let them complain.

As I plugged in my headset jack and began logging onto the various systems and terminals, I remembered the tiny earthquake we had once. We were backed up over a hundred calls. People were calling us from all over the county.

"Nine-one-one center," I'd said.

"I think we just had an earthquake."

"Do you need police, fire or ambulance?"

"Me? No. I don't. But I'm pretty sure we just had an earthquake."

"Are you all right?"

"I'm fine, yes."

"Ma'am, why are you calling nine-one-one?"

"Because, I told you, I think we just had an earthquake."

"If you're all set, ma'am, I have to answer more emergency calls. Are you all set, ma'am?"

"I, um. Yes. I guess I am."

Call after call came in like that. Eventually, we answered them all, and called back all the people who called in, but hung-up. It goes like that all the time. That doesn't stop squeaky wheels from demanding their oil.

Once logged in, I glanced at the prompter. We were now thirty calls in queue. I went Ready. Phone rang. I answered it. "Nine-one-one center?"

"There's been an accident, a car rolled over. It's off the expressway. I didn't see anyone get out. No one got out."

"Sir, where did this happen?"

"On the expressway," the caller said.

"Sir, there are three different expressways."

"It's right here on the expressway I'm on. It's…four-ninety," he said.

I-490 ran east and west, from LeRoy to Victor. "Sir, four-ninety is 37 miles long. Can you be more specific? Which direction are you traveling?"

"I'm headed toward the city. I can see the city from where I am."

"Sir, this is very important. Whether you are going east or west, you will be headed toward the city. What is the exit you just passed, or the exit you are coming to?"

"I don't see an exit. We're between exits," he said.

I kept re-bidding his cell phone, trying to triangulate the

location to as close as possible to where he was. When I tried pulling up the information, all I was saw was a single cell tower, which told me absolutely nothing. "Sir, what was the last exit you passed?"

"It was snowing too hard, I'm not sure. I couldn't see."

I muted my headset. "Supervisor!"

Milzy came over to my pod of telecommunicators. "What have you got, McKinney?"

"Caller witnessed a rollover somewhere on four-ninety. He has no clue where he is, which direction, and--"

"Rebid the call?"

"--re-bidding isn't finding him."

Milzy called out, "Anyone have a vehicle rollover on four-ninety?"

"Event thirty-seven-twenty-eight," someone said.

I looked at that event, nodded at Milzy that I was all set, and un-muted my headset, "Sir, what color was the vehicle that rolled?"

"Ah, it was a red SUV. I pulled over. I don't feel safe though. Cars are sliding all over the place."

I read through the job. Saw that one of the other telecommunicators who took the call indicated a red SUV had rolled off onto the median, people trapped. Fire, police and ambulances were already on the way.

"Sir, I want you to do what is safest for you. If you don't want to remain pulled over, then don't," I said.

"So I should leave?"

"I'm saying it's up to *you*, sir. Whatever you feel safest doing, you should do," I said, and asked him his name and then for his phone number.

"I'm calling from my cell phone."

"I understand that. What is the *phone* number?" I verified with him that the location for the event was near the same location where he was initially pulled over.

I disconnected that call, and was about to go available for the next call, when sitting up at the supervisor pod, Milzy called my name. "Can you come up here for a second?"

I removed my headset, stood and glanced around the room.

Still in queue, I wondered what was up. Supervisors listened in on some calls. Quality control and all of that. They had to grade a number of calls per employee each month. I'd been here minutes, we were busy, and on overtime. Milzy wouldn't call me up to the pod unless it had to do with something else, something more substantial.

"What's up?" I said, taking the two steps up to enter the pod. The telecommunicator, fire and EMS and police dispatchers encircled the supervisors who sat in the center of the operations floor.

"Come here," he said. He motioned with a finger, and pulled out the chair next to him. "You're going to want to sit down for this."

Sit down? I tried to swallow, couldn't. "What's going on?"

"It's about you," he said. I stared at his face, looking for any hint of a smile that this was all a gag.

"Me?"

"I hate to tell you this. There's no easy way to say it," he said.

"Milzy, just cut the shit. What's going on?"

"Your daughter has something to tell you," Milzy said, and looked across the small table. I followed his gaze.

Charlene wore a 9-1-1 uniform. That powder blue shirt, the collar brass complete with a badge and a nameplate with my dead son's name on it that simply read: CASH MCKINNEY.

"Char, what--Milzy, what's she doing here?"

Charlene reached across the table and set her hand on top of mine. "Daddy, you're dead...Daddy. You're dead. Daddy! Daddy!"

CHAPTER SEVEN

"Daddy! Daddy!"

When my eyes opened, I tried to jump forward. Something had me around the chest, holding me back. I screamed, struggling against it in an attempt to free myself.

"You're having a nightmare, Dad. It's okay. You're okay."

"Chase!" Allison unfastened a seat belt, knelt in front of me. "It was a bad dream. It's okay."

I know my eyes were opened wide. I looked around. At first, I thought I saw computer terminals from work and people around me in blue uniforms. The scene melted into a row of seats a couple of feet across from where I sat. Dave stared at me. Sues had her head on his chest. He still brushed her hair with his hand, with his bloody hand. We were on a plane, headed south. I got it. It came back. "How long was I asleep?"

"Almost an hour, Dad," Charlene said.

I unfastened my seatbelt and stood up, helping Allison to her feet. "I'm okay," I said. "Sit back down. Buckle up. I'm going to check on our pilots."

"Okay." Allison sat back down, but in my seat, next to my daughter. She wasted no time securing herself to the chair. They snuggled close.

"I'll be right back. You guys good?" They nodded. "Dave, you need anything?"

He shook his head. "I'm okay. I don't know, a blanket? Water, if you can find any?"

Water. Food. We'd need both, and soon. "I'll see what I can find."

There really wasn't anywhere to look. We were on a plane. If there was water anywhere, it would be around where they were all seated. I saw some strapped down boxes along the sides, by the very tail. I'd explore them once I made sure Palmeri and Erway were good.

I stood just outside the cockpit. Our pilots chatted, laughing. "Ladies," I said.

Erway jumped, and spun around. "Scared me, Chase."

"Didn't mean to, sorry about that." I held up my hands and smiled. "Wish I bore gifts. Like coffee."

"Coffee," Palmeri said, and moaned. "A cup would be amazing right now."

"A pot," Erway said.

"A pot." Palmeri nodded.

"How we doing?" I said.

Palmeri cocked her head to one side. "Pretty smooth. Take-off went well. Thing's a box, but it flies nice. I'm keeping at just over two hundred miles an hour, and just under ten thousand feet. I go too high, we won't just be cold, we'll need oxygen masks."

Might explain why I fell asleep so easily. Lack of oxygen. It was that or just sheer exhaustion. "I'm going to search the plane, look for blankets and water, or for anything useful."

"Sounds good." Erway gave me a thumb's up. "And, hey, if you find any coffee--"

"I know, I know. I'll pour you two the first cups."

"Holy shit, I don't believe it," Palmeri said.

I stuck my head forward between them. "What?"

Palmeri didn't speak. She pointed to her far left and slowly followed the airplane about to pass by us. "That a commercial airline?"

"Yes. Yes it is," Palmeri said. "A seven-forty-seven."

"We going to hit them?"

"No, they're at least two thousand feet above us, and they're pretty far away." Palmeri still readjusted her grip on the wheel. "Just where the fuck are they going?"

"Can we ask them?" I said, and pointed at the radio.

"Can try," Palmeri said.

"They must see us too, right?" Erway strained against her seatbelt, as if the extra half an inch would give her a better view of the passing airplane.

Palmeri snatched up the handheld radio that resembled a C.B. "This is Sherpa to the Boeing seven-four-seven, Sherpa to Boeing…"

Static. Nothing. Palmeri looked at me, and shrugged. She tried again.

More static. "I don't think--"

"Sherpa, this is Boeing seven-four-seven, over."

My hand went to my stomach. Thought I might heave. I knew we weren't alone, the only non-infected humans left on the planet, but for a moment, I did believe we might be the only ones in the sky.

"Boeing, we have you in sight. Over."

"And we see you, Sherpa. How many souls on board? Over."

"Seven, seven total. You? Over."

"Forty-eight, Sherpa. We have a total of forty-eight. Over."

Palmeri looked back at me, nodding. "Damn."

"Boeing, what is your destination? Over."

Silence. Static.

"Sherpa, no offense meant, but our destination is confidential. We don't know you. Based on things we've seen, we're inclined to keep pertinent information to ourselves. Over."

"They don't trust us. Worried we might follow them. Attack their family," I said.

"Trust is going to be an issue for a while," Erway said.

I thought about Josh, Dave's brother. He'd been shot and killed. Shot. A senseless death by someone with a gun. I'd still love to get my hands on the ones responsible. Part of me believed we should be gathering as survivors and joining forces. At some point in time, we'd need to rebuild. Install government. Figure out how to regain electricity, power and run nuclear plants, and operate water purification plants. Holy shit. It was going to be a daunting task. "I don't blame them."

"Sherpa to Boeing, we copy. Wish you a safe flight. Safe landing. Over."

A pause. Static. "We extend our best wishes your way, as well, Sherpa. Be safe. Out."

Palmeri set the hand-held down. Kept her hand on it. "I think I'd have felt better not having seen them."

"Why is that?" I said.

"I kind of want to join them," she said.

"We don't know where they're headed," Erway said.

"And they don't want us," I said.

"How are we going to make it out of this," Palmeri said. "I mean, they're flying north. We're headed south-west. They think the grass is greener in Canada or the North Pole, and we think the equator. There are probably survivors in Georgia headed to Seattle, and people in L.A. trekking toward Manhattan. Who's right, you know? Who's wrong?"

There was some comfort in knowing these thoughts and that the questions didn't just run through my mind. The bad part was that no one had any answers. The Boeing might have an idea flying north. Colder temperatures might slow the zombies down. Rain and water seemed to annoy them. There was a good chance snow might be a hundred times better as a natural weapon. I couldn't deny it. Boeing had me second guessing Mexico.

I mean, *Mexico*. The thought came to me over a week ago, back when this all started. When Allison and I were fleeing the 9-1-1 Center. It was something someone had said on a radio station about how Mexico *might* be a safe bet because they didn't have flu vaccinations to inoculate their people, not like America had. Then there was the wall. The one we'd built to keep illegal immigrants out of our country. That would be an awesome fortress to keep us safe, once on the Mexican side, from the infected Americans.

That's what I'd thought then. It was the one thing that I held onto. "I don't know why we're going to Mexico. I really don't."

"You told us why. We agree with you," Erway said. "If I didn't think you were on to something, I'd not have hung around."

I bit my lip. "You don't get it though. I could be wrong. As wrong as the Boeing headed north, or the L.A. people going to Manhattan. Mexico might not be any safer than it was for us up along the St. Lawrence. This thing, this disease, it keeps spreading. For all I know, we're going to cross that border, God willing, and it will end up like stepping across the threshold into hell."

"We won't blame you for trying," Palmeri said. "I've got nothing better, no more answers than anyone else, but like Erway said, there's something solid about your plan. Way I see it, the way *we* see it because we talked about it while you were back there, the key to surviving might be just to keep moving. This disease, or infection isn't going to end anytime soon. The millions affected, we have to get rid of them. How do you get rid of millions of people? Where to you dispose of them? They're going to need to be disposed of, aren't they? And the thing is, I don't think it's gotten as bad as it's going to get. I think, we think, moving, as long as we *keep* moving, is going to be the only way to make it. And right now, we're headed to Mexico."

"That's, ah, that's a lot I hadn't thought of," I said. I remembered the things about the zombies, the almost human-like qualities exhibited, and that I still needed to share all of that with the others. We'd not had the time to sit around and talk.

I walked out of the cockpit area and held a hand out, placing it against the bathroom door for balance. It wasn't Palmeri's flying that had me wobbling. My mind was in the midst of a whirlwind of so many thoughts that I thought my legs might give out.

I needed to pare down the things in my brain. I whittled it away to just two as best I could. The other thoughts were still there, whipping around like debris in the funnel of a tornado, but I was able to focus. What I concentrated on were blankets and water.

CHAPTER EIGHT

Seemed like there had been more than two large wooden boxes in the hold. There were just the two set at the end of the rows of seats.

"Need a hand?" Allison stood.

"Stay buckled up. I just want to see if there's any supplies we can use on this plane," I said. I thought about telling the others about the Boeing. I wasn't sure if that would boost or cripple morale. For now, the best thing to do seemed to be keeping it to myself.

On top of one crate was a crowbar. Both crates were strapped to pallets. I loosened the straps on one and drove the curved end of the bar into the top. I pried at the lid, working my way around each side. The board creaked and moaned in protest.

"Chase," Allison said.

"I got it," I said. "It's giving."

"Chase," she said, again.

"Dad!"

I turned around.

Dave unbuckled his seatbelt. He knelt in front of Sues. "No," he said. "No, no. No."

Ah shit. I kept the crowbar in my hand. Sues had been dying for some time now, slowly. She must have been in pain. She'd lost a lot of blood, both on the tarmac, and while we'd been on the plane. The pool puddled below her seat made that apparent. I don't know how long it took once a person died before they turned. I still wasn't convinced it happened to everyone upon death. My experience with this aspect of the disease was limited. "Dave, are you all right?"

"It shouldn't have happened to her. She shouldn't have been out there driving that thing, pulling us out of the hangar. What had I been thinking? I mean, fuck. Fuck!"

"It's not your fault, buddy. There's nothing we could have done."

Dave stood up. Sues' head fell forward. Blood, thick and dark, oozed from her gaping mouth. "There is something I could have done." He pointed a finger hard against his chest. "She didn't have to be the one to drive that buggy. I could have done it. I could have opened the door. I could have pulled the plane out. I should have. Me."

We'd had this talk. I felt the same way. I thought I should be doing everything, and felt responsible for everyone. "Dave," I said.

"No, Chase. No."

"Dad, she's moving," Charlene said. She unbuckled her belt.

I held up a hand, stopping her. "Dave," I said.

He wasn't listening to me. He stared at Sues. Her eyes opened. Her head slowly rose off her chest. She snarled and screamed. Her hands shot forward, fingers reaching for a catch on Dave.

He cried, shoulders shaking, head bowed. He ran his hand through his hair.

Charlene walked around Dave and stood next to me. "Dad," she said, with a hand on the hilt of her sword.

I shook my head at her, and tried again. "Dave."

He took one staggering step toward Sues. I wish I knew what was going on inside his head, what he was thinking. Part of me expected him to take a knee in front of his girlfriend and simply surrender. "David!"

He looked up at me. The tears cleaned the dirt in trails snaking down his cheeks. "You're not touching her. You. Are. Not. Touching. Her!"

I kept an arm in front of my daughter. I sensed her muscles tense, like she might be ready to strike.

"Dave," I said. "You can't leave her like this."

The scene was seared into my memory. She thrust her arms

and shoulders, as she struggled from side-to-side and back and forth against the seat belt which now, thankfully, worked like a restraint. The cackles she emitted bounced around the shell of the inside of the plane. The screams competed with the droning whine of the engines.

"You are not going to kill her, McKinney. You're not!" He pulled out a handgun. He aimed it at me, and swung around, pointing it at everyone.

"Are you kidding me, Dave? Are you out of your fucking mind?" I took another step toward him, and in front of my daughter. "Put the gun down."

Dave didn't listen. He didn't lower his gun. He aimed it, not at me, not at Charlene or Allison, and not at Sues. He tipped his head back and pointed the short barrel under his chin. "There's no point, Chase. I mean, really, is there? We go here. We go there. What's the point?"

"We all feel that way, David. We all do, but we can't give up. We can't just, just…quit."

"I have nothing left, Chase. Nothing. Josh is dead. Sues…" he said. He strained to look at her, and looked away. "None of this is going to get better."

"It will, Dave. It has to," I said.

"It has to? What the fuck does that mean? It doesn't have to, it doesn't ever have to. This country, this world, this planet, it's sick. It doesn't have to do shit to get better. I don't think I can do it anymore. I can't just keep doing this. I don't want to keep doing this. I don't," he said. The crying came out in sobs. His words were tough to understand. I followed, though.

"We all feel that, Dave. You are not alone."

Dave lowered the gun, pointing it at Sues. "Yes. I am."

I held up my hands and stepped closer. "We're going to get through this together."

"That's what she thought," he said. "That we'd get through this together. I know it sounds stupid, man. It's stupid, but I loved her."

"It's not stupid," I said. It wasn't stupid at all. "We're not alone. We're not the last survivors. Just a minute ago, before I came back here, we saw another plane."

"What?" Charlene said. "There was another plane?"

"Yes, another plane." I nodded. "We talked to them. A big plane that was headed north. They wouldn't tell us where, but they were up here in the sky with us. Things are bad, may get worse, but we're not alone. We're not. There is a chance we can fix this. Rebuild. Start over. Dave, everything's not lost. It's not."

"There's no hope, McKinney."

"There is. It's dim, but it's there."

He shook his head. "I don't think--"

The plane must have hit a pocket of turbulence. We dropped quickly, and tipped left then right.

Dave lost his balance and fell into Sues.

She wasted no time wrapping her arms around him, attempting to pull him toward her mouth. Dark drool dangled from her lower lip. Her clouded-over eyes were open wide as she prepared to bite him.

I'd fallen back and into Charlene, who went down under my weight.

Allison looked stunned and paralyzed. She held onto her seat belt with both hands, as if making sure it was tight around her waist. Her eyes were squeezed shut.

"Honey, are you okay?" I said, and struggled to regain my balance. "Dave!"

"Fine. I'm fine," Charlene said.

Dave locked his hands with Sues, like they might play that childhood game where you bend fingers back until someone screamed *pinochle* to end the pain and torment. This was no game. I felt thankful Dave was fighting back, if only to maintain his own survival.

The plane rocked, tipping to the left side.

Dave's head, his neck, were a breath away from Sues' wide-opened mouth.

Then I thought, *he's going to let her bite him*. I found my feet and ran as best I could toward them, the crowbar raised.

The plane teetered back and forth before finally leveling out.

The teetering knocked me toward the opposite side of the plane, next to the last seat in the row Allison sat in. I fell hard, my elbow hitting the side of the first crate. Pain shot both up and down my arm. The funny bone. I was not laughing. Tears filled my eyes. "Dave!"

As I managed to get onto my knees, the gun fired. Sues' head flew back as bits of hair and skin, skull and brain painted the inside plane wall in a graphic spattering.

Dave dropped the gun. He lay flat on his stomach.

I scrambled over to him, and lifted his head. "Dave?"

He was crying, lips quivered, his hands were balled into fists. I placed his head on my lap, and held it there. I kept his head in my lap while he cried.

CHAPTER NINE

"Chase!"

I looked up. Erway called from the cockpit. "Charlene, can you see what they want? Tell them, ah, tell them what just happened back here."

She walked cautiously, slow and steady steps, from the back of the plane to the front. "I got it, Dad."

Dave's crying had stopped. He kept his head on my lap. I don't think he had it in him to move. I made eye contact with Allison. She chewed on the skin around her thumb and shook her head.

Everyone seemed ready to give up.

"Dad, they said we're low on fuel. The Pittsburgh International Airport isn't far. Elysia wants to try to make it there and land."

I nodded. "Sounds like a plan."

Charlene relayed my agreement. "She says we should all get buckled in again, because it could be a rough landing, *if* we have enough fuel, and it could be a fuck of a time if we don't."

"Charlene," I said.

"Just telling *you* what she told *me*."

"Go strap in next to Allison." I lifted Dave's head off my legs and set it down gently. I stood and walked over to the crates. Behind the first one was a tarp. I pulled on it. It ripped on one corner that had been stuck under the edge of the pallet. It would still suffice. I draped the tarp over Sues' remains.

I slipped my arms under Dave's, and lifted him up. "You've got to help me, buddy. We need to get you into a chair."

"Want me to help, Dad?"

"No, keep that seat belt on." I stood, kept my arms under his and dragged him toward the front area of the plane. There was no way I could lift him into a seat. "Dave, you've got to help me, man, okay?"

I didn't expect any response, but Dave placed his hands on the seat and hoisted himself up and into it. I grabbed the ends of the seat belt and secured him in place. "We're getting through this," I said.

"You guys buckled in?" Erway said.

I went to the cockpit.

"Why aren't you seated," she said. "Go, get locked in. We're not going to make the airport."

"Palmeri?"

"Fuel's just about gone. We've got too much distance to cover. I thought we might make it, but now, I'm not so sure."

"What are we going to do?"

"I'm keeping an eye out for I-79. Figure if there's a good stretch of open road it might work."

"Our expressways were littered with abandoned and disabled vehicles," I said. "Couldn't even drive on them. How are we going to land a plane?"

"Go put on your seatbelt."

The plane shuddered. I looked back. Palmeri had her arm up, throwing toggles and pushing buttons on the panel over her head.

I sat between Allison and Charlene. "How is he?" I motioned toward Dave, as I buckled the belt.

"What's going on up there?" Allison said.

Dave sat with one arm folded, his face buried in a hand. I thought he was going to take his life. I actually feared he'd been a heartbeat away from blowing out his brains. We needed a break here, a chance to regroup.

"Chase? What's going on up there?"

"We're just low on fuel," I said, hoping it sounded light and non-important.

"Are we about to crash? Did they tell you that? That we're

going to crash?"

"Palmeri's not sure if there's enough fuel to reach the airport."

"So we're about to crash. I knew it. I knew getting in this thing was like signing our own…" She stopped talking, cut herself off, and looked over at Dave.

"Palmeri knows what she's doing. She's going to land us somewhere just as safe," I said. "We don't have anything to worry about."

"Running out of fuel a million miles up in the air? Why would I worry about that? I mean, what did Palmeri tell us? She had a hundred hours of flying experience in what? A Cessna? I'm not worried, Chase. I'm not freaking out." She crossed her legs, folded her arms and turned her head. Then, she unfolded her arms, uncrossed her legs and looked directly at me. "Where is she planning on landing the plane, Chase? Did she tell you that?"

"I-79," I said.

Charlene rolled her eyes, as if silently calling me crazy for being so honest. Then she sighed for punctuation.

I didn't know where we were over Pennsylvania, or how far the airport was. I didn't know how long we flew in silence waiting to land. I kept looking at Dave, and then at Sues. I held one of Allison's hands, and one of my daughter's and felt guilty.

"We're going to be landing!" It was Erway, a shout from the cockpit. Part of me wanted to go look out a window. There were a few, but none near where we were seated.

Allison and Charlene both squeezed my hands. I squeezed back and stared at Dave. He hadn't moved, his face still in his hand.

The plane bounced up and down as we began the descent, tipping left and right. I closed my eyes tight and remembered things I wanted to forget.

# # #

I'd gathered up some things and stuffed them into a duffel bag. I looked around the bedroom. Looked at the items on the dressers. It felt surreal. My stomach, knotted, threatened to explode. That was what had made it real. Too real. I was going to be sick.

I walked with my bag into the living room which held a big screen television, sofas and a recliner. With the exception of a large clock that matched the motif, an array of framed photographs of Charlene and Cash decorated the walls.

Charlene stood there staring at me. I sat on the sofa and placed her on my lap. I thought at the age of nine, she'd never understand what was really going on. She'd know something was wrong, but it wouldn't mean anything to her. It wouldn't impact her.

I looked at Julie, who was on the loveseat with Cash on her knees. She couldn't meet my eyes, and looked away. She wasn't going to say anything. It was going to be up to me to explain. I hated her. I really did. I hated her for so many reasons, but right now, I hated her most for this.

"For a little while, honey, Daddy's going to go and stay someplace else," I said. Toughest words to ever come out of my mouth.

I expected her to say, "Why, Daddy?" or "Okay, can I play now?"

Charlene's head just dropped and the tears were immediate. "No," she said.

I put my arm around her little shoulders. She fell into me and cried.

Cash looked at his sister and touched a finger to his mouth, like he was thinking. He was only four years old. "Mommy?" he said.

"Daddy and I need some time apart," she said. Cash wasn't going to get it. He couldn't. Not at four.

"Daddy isn't going to leave," he said.

Charlene shook as she cried. Her tears felt hot as they soaked through my shirt. "No, Daddy. I don't want you to go," she said. "I don't want you to leave."

I wasn't going. I wasn't leaving. She was making me. I couldn't say that. I couldn't point fingers. The kids didn't need that. They didn't need to be in the middle of anything, especially shit caused by their parents. "I'm not going far." I was crying, too.

Hard. I held my daughter, and couldn't wipe away my tears.

We stayed that way, on the couch, holding our crying kids for nearly thirty minutes. Cash cried himself to sleep.

When I stood up, Charlene in my arms, I kissed Cash on the top of the head before Julie laid him down on the cushions.

I hugged Charlene tight. She wrapped her legs around my waist, like she knew what was next. That I'd have to set her down, and about to walk out the front door and *leave*. That I was *going*.

"I've got to go for now," I said.

She squeezed me with her legs. Her arms around my neck cut off my air.

Julie put her hands on Charlene in an attempt to remove her.

I spun away. "I got this," I said, seething.

"Stay with us, Daddy." It was whispered over and over in my ear.

I don't remember setting her down, or handing her over to her mother. I don't remember walking out the door and getting into my car. My brain blocked out that portion of the memory. A possible defense mechanism that kept me from losing my mind. I don't remember anything until I found myself in a gas station parking lot buying my first pack of cigarettes in nearly a decade.

Their voices begging me not to go, and to stay home with them has haunted me from that moment on. It reoccurred in nightmares. I heard it always for years. Still hear it all of the time, and it is always like a machete chopping through my chest and splitting my heart in half.

Then their mother was a zombie on a bed, crawling toward me. I was swinging the edge of a shovel at her head. Her skull was splitting open and spraying gunk all over hardwood floors.

CHAPTER TEN

I opened my eyes when my stomach dropped. I opened them wide. My mouth was open wide, as well. I think Charlene and Allison were both screaming, but it was hard to tell for sure over the sound of my own screams. I didn't think the descent should have occurred so abruptly. The plane jostled up and down and from side to side. We were either hitting pockets of turbulence, or we were not just low on fuel, but out.

Someone yelled, "Brace yourselves!"

I still held both my daughter and girlfriend's hands. I knew I might be squeezing too tightly, but could not help it, could not stop. I was scared; terrified. The fact that it felt like we'd been falling for several minutes, and continued falling, was disheartening to say the very least. With each foot we fell, we picked up speed. I wondered if my stomach would stop dropping. It didn't. Catching my breath was difficult, except for screaming. And we continued to, what felt like plummeting towards earth.

I kept thinking about the landing gear. Did it go up when we took off? Had it been lowered as we fell? Were we pointing straight down? Would we just smash and explode on impact?

Closing my eyes and keeping them closed made the most sense. I couldn't do it. I needed to see what was happening. I did not like not being in control. Sitting back here and not up at the controls irritated my OCD.

I turned my head to look at my daughter. Her eyes were tightly shut. Her mouth was pulled down into a frown, and then opened wide into an O. She might be screaming, but I couldn't tell. I could not hear her over the whine of engines. I wanted to hold her, hug her. She shouldn't die this way, should never have to live through something this catastrophic either. No one deserved it, but she didn't deserve it the most.

Allison's fingernails dug into the top of my hand and drew blood.

Then we smashed into the earth. The seatbelt pulled tight against my waist, and I felt the air launched from my lungs in a pained gasp. My head rocked back, slammed into the wall of the inside of the plane. Something exploded through the floor of the plane only a foot away from Sues' corpse, protruding up like a malfunctioned missile. The plane tipped to the left, toward her. I knew what it was that stuck up from the base: part of the landing gear. Despite being bounced back and forth, I saw the wheel. It wasn't rolling. It was, instead, wedged. Sparks like fireworks sprayed inside the plane.

We were spinning and sliding along the ground.

We hit something hard. This sent the plane spinning in the opposite direction as simultaneously rivets popped and metal tore as the left part of the hull ripped open and peeled away from the plane. Everything and anything loose was sucked toward and out the opening.

We continued to spin, shake and bounce. I saw something like welding sparks split the nighttime darkness, and realized I was looking at the wing tumble and roll away. This felt surreal and seemed to unroll in slow motion. All I could think was, *did I just see the wing* severed *from the body.*

Thankfully, seatbelts held us securely in place.

I didn't think we'd explode since we didn't have fuel. This did little to calm the fear and flooding emotions.

Then…it was over.

We'd come to a grinding stop. My ears rang. The sound of metal on, what I believed to be asphalt reverberated between my ears. I thought I might be deaf, and that the screeching might never subside, but we'd lived through a plane crash. Only thing I could think, ironically enough was, *"Add that to my bucket list."*

# # #

Despite wanting to sit still, eyes closed and take deep breaths until my heartbeat slowed to normal, I unfastened my seatbelt and dropped to my knees in front of my daughter. "Charlene," I said.

She did not move. Eyes closed. My heart almost stopped. "Char?"

I put my hands on her shoulders, and gently shook her.

Her head lolled from side to side. "Honey?"

"Chase?" Allison winced. Her hands fumbled with her seatbelt. She seemed unable to unfasten it. I saw the blood on the part of the plane behind her head. She must have smacked her skull good.

"Daddy," Charlene said.

I unfastened her belt, leaning forward to hug my daughter. "Scared me, honey. God, you scared me."

She was crying, her fingers curling into fists in my hair.

Allison managed to get free of her belt, stood, and fell forward.

"Alley," I said, and had to reluctantly pull away from my daughter. I knelt beside Allison. "Hey, Alley?"

Her eyes were open. "I got dizzy."

Had to be a concussion. I wasn't sure how to verify it. Too dark inside the plane to check her eyes, wasn't sure what I'd look for even if there had been better lighting.

Dave.

I looked to my right. Dave was just getting out of his seat. He looked as battered and beaten up as I felt. "Hey, buddy, you okay?"

Dave shrugged. "I guess. How are you guys? Allison?"

"A little woozy," she said, and laughed.

Charlene stood up, stretched out her legs. "Should I check on our pilots?"

"I'll do that. You stay with your dad." Dave walked past us, not with steady legs. His knees wobbled and he held his arms out for balance. He may have hit his head as well. Two concussions. Fucking wonderful.

Charlene knelt on the opposite side of Allison. "Where are we?"

"I don't know, honey," I said. I figured we were someplace in Pennsylvania. I don't think we made it to the Pittsburgh Airport. If we did, we'd just done a job to the tarmac.

"Ah, Chase?" Dave leaned into our area of the plane and waved me over. Couldn't be good. Being cryptic wasn't going to hide anything from Allison and Charlene, either. One or both of the pilots were dead. I knew it without going to look in on them, and they knew it. I stood up and walked toward the cockpit.

"What have we got?" I said.

He shook his head. "It's not good."

I walked past him and peeked into the cockpit, and nearly shrank back a step. A shiver slid down my back as if a skeleton's icy finger had traced my spine.

I did not expect to see so much blood.

"Don't worry about me, not me. Check on her." Palmeri sucked in a deep breath and winced.

I reached around as best I could and placed my fingers on Erway's neck, feeling for a pulse. I pressed my fingers hard against clammy skin, blood soaked skin. "I'm not getting anything," I said. I didn't remove my hand. I moved to a different location, tilted my head to the side and closed my eyes, like that might help me feel for the pulse better. It didn't, I still could not find one.

The front windshield was smashed out. Debris littered the cockpit. Her head was not split. The wound had to be somewhere else on her body and I couldn't see it. It didn't matter. She was dead.

"She's gone," I said. "Let's get you out of that seat."

Palmeri nodded, lips pursed. She looked down. "Don't think that's going to be easy."

What looked like a metal shaft protruded out of her thigh. "Ah shit."

I'd said that out loud. Hadn't meant to.

"Exactly," she said. She offered something to me. A pocket flashlight. I took it and saw her tears and her lip quivered. She seemed to be fighting the urge to cry. I wasn't sure why. If there was ever a time to ball, this was it. This was definitely it.

"I'll be right back."

Dave stood with his back to the wall between the cockpit and the area where Allison and Charlene were. "Erway's dead," I said. "And Palmeri, she's pinned with a shaft through her thigh. Thick shaft. Only way to get her out is to lift her directly off the shaft, straight up. Cockpit's cramped as fuck. Don't think that's going to work. And, if we do, good chance something inside is severed and then she'll bleed out fast, know what I'm saying?"

Dave looked thoughtful for a moment. "Maybe under the plane we'll get a better view. If we can free the shaft, then she just keeps it in her leg until we find a safe way to remove it?"

"Yeah, I don't know. That makes sense," I said.

"It makes sense to at least try it if we can't think of anything else," he said.

"I'll check under the plane. You keep an eye on her. She might go into shock. I looked for blankets earlier. There's that tarp, maybe some other things we can use to keep her warm," I said.

Dave nodded.

I clapped a hand onto his shoulder and opened my mouth.

He stopped me. "We're good, man. I'm good."

He wasn't good. I was glad to hear that we were, at least. "Okay, buddy. Okay."

"Hey, Chase?"

I stopped.

"Remember one thing while you're out there," he said.

"What's that?"

"We just crashed a plane. We're going to attract a lot of attention. Zombies, and whatever. You know?"

CHAPTER ELEVEN

Butler County, Pennsylvania, 2019 hours

I touched the hilt of my sword and knife and felt the weight, light as it was, of the machete in its sheath across my back.

"Where are you going?" Charlene stood beside me. Seemed to come out of nowhere. I was by the door to get off the plane. Could just have easily walked out of the gaping hole on the side.

"I need to check something," I said.

"What are we checking?"

"Not we. I need you to stay here," I said.

"I'm going with you," she said.

"I'd let you, but I need you to keep an eye on Allison. Otherwise, you could."

"She's fine."

Allison was still flat on her back. "She has a concussion. She might start throwing up or she could go into shock, too."

"Too?"

"Palmeri. She's injured pretty bad. Dave's keeping an eye on her." Dave walked past us.

Charlene grunted.

"He's looking for blankets, or anything that will keep Palmeri and Allison warm. We don't want either of them going into shock."

"I'll keep an eye on her, but if she starts throwing up--"

"Honey, we need to be together on this, on things. I hate vomit as much as you do." Changing diapers never bothered me, but I was a *sympathy* puker. Someone loses their lunch, mine isn't far behind. Charlene was the same way. Smell alone could start me yakking. "People need our help, and we're lucky to be well enough to give it. Do you understand that? We might not always be as healthy as we are right now. If that were you or me lying there, wouldn't you want someone looking out for us? I'm not just shooting smoke. I'm not feeding you a line. We need to look out for each other. We need to," I said.

"I got it, Dad. I'll keep an eye on her. And, I'm sorry."

I pulled her head to my chest. Kissed the top of it. "No need. We all need reminding every once in a while. I know I do, too."

She pulled away. "You didn't say anything about Johanna. She all right?"

I had to think a second. Johanna Erway. "She didn't make it, honey."

Charlene looked at me. At that moment, I knew she got it. She understood what we'd just talked about; looking out for one another. If we didn't do this one simple thing, we'd never survive.

If we didn't do this simple thing, and did survive, what would be the point?

"I'll be right back," I said.

"Be careful." Charlene gave me a kiss on the cheek and went to help Dave free the tarp behind the crates. I watched for just a brief moment longer and then pushed open the door. The flashlight would be necessary once under the front of the plane. I didn't want to turn it on too soon. The light would shine like a beacon in the darkness.

Dave was right. A plane crash was going to attract attention.

I stepped off the plane and looked around, squinting to see anything. It appeared to be a long stretch of road. It wasn't an interstate. That much, I could tell. I felt disorientated, didn't know which direction I faced. Best I could do was left and right. Be nice if lights worked. Looked as if we were mostly surrounded by trees, but not exactly. Something was to my left. A building--a small row of them. Resembled more of a structural shadow in what little light did come from the sky.

I stayed close to the plane, one hand on it, as I made the short walk to the front. My eyes never stopped scanning the area. If we were alone, thank God. If not, I hoped I'd catch movement with enough time to react, and worse case, warn the others. I removed the long sword from the scabbard affixed to my belt.

The darkness was unnerving. Seemed to continually swallow up space around me. Each step I took, the step before was swallowed into nothing. Each step I was about to take appeared to be into a black void. Brought back childhood memories, fears, actually. The trick at bedtime was to turn off the light and cross the distance between the switch and the bed without touching the floor. The floor was not the problem, it was the apprehension behind whatever monster lurked underneath the box spring, because at six, seven, hell at ten, there was always something lying in wait.

It was that feeling that I felt now, overwhelmingly so. I needed to find a way to free Palmeri and then make it back inside the plane in a single leap, or risk being snatched by whatever monster lurked in the darkness that surrounded me.

Decidedly, I thrust the long sword back into the scabbard and lit the flashlight Palmeri gave me and tried to cup and aim the light using most of the palm of my hand. The little beam brought a false consolation that I tried to embrace completely.

The light played over the plane. There were holes all over the front of it. I couldn't see into the cockpit from where I stood, because it was a little too high off the ground. From where I stood, I could see under it. More than that, I could also see up into it. There I unleashed all the LED power of the flashlight, and the inside of the plane glowed from it.

With no tools, even if I could figure out how to free Palmeri from under here, I wasn't sure I would be able. The bent and ripped apart metal was sharp, and I couldn't fit up inside. I could reach in, but in doing so, could no longer see what I was doing. "Dave?"

"We see the light," he said.

That didn't help any. "I'm going to try to move things around. If I find the bottom half of what's in your leg, Palmeri, it's probably going to hurt pretty good, you know? Tell me when you're ready."

"I'm ready," she said.

I grabbed onto whatever I could and tugged. There was no give. The plane might be wrecked, but twisted metal seemed just as hard to wiggle as untwisted metal. "Anything?"

There was a moment of silence, and then, "No."

I released whatever I'd gripped and tried a different handhold. "Now?"

"No, nothing. This isn't going to work," she said.

I heard Dave. "It'll work. It'll work. If anyone can help, it's McKinney."

Wish he hadn't said that. Didn't need that kind of pressure. I turned off the flashlight, dropped it into my pocket and reached into the hole in the bottom of the plane with both arms raised. I was able to fit my head and shoulders up into the opening as well. Felt like I was climbing up into the Rabbit Hole, until sharp metal sliced through my body. It cut from under my left arm to the edge of my ribcage. "Son of a fucking bitch!"

"Chase?"

"I'm good, Dave. I'm alright." Warm blood oozed from the wound. I felt it roll down my side. There was plenty to grab onto, so I did. One by one, I attempted pushing and pulling whatever I could, mostly to no avail. "Anything, anything at all?"

"No, Chase, nothing," Dave said.

I didn't give up. I kept at it, reaching deeper, higher, and all around me. There was a lot of things under here that could be attached to the shaft that pierced Palmeri.

"Chase?"

"I'm trying," I said, but claustrophobia was sneaking up on me. My breathing became quick and shallow, and despite the chill in the November mountain air, I was sweating. It hadn't been that long ago that I signed up to be a volunteer fireman. Being divorced, I was plagued with too much free time on my hands. The days and nights that I didn't have my kids could be time better spent. I knew this much. Volunteering seemed like a good way to find something constructive to do with my excess of time. I joined an agency, passed the physical and agility tests, and was sworn in

66

to the department.

The way I saw it, I worked on one side of the radio and sent rescuers to various emergencies. It would be interesting seeing what first responding was like. During my SCBA July training, I had to don complete turnout gear; the pants with suspenders, the boots, the jacket, the hooded face mask, jacket, gloves and helmet, and then shrug on an air tank with 30 minutes of air inside that I'd breathe using a mask. I was handed an axe and told to follow my instructor. The purpose was to use up all the air in the tank. It had to be ninety degrees outside, fifty times hotter with the turnout gear on. We walked all around the outside perimeter of the firehouse, into the firehouse and down into the basement, then up to the roof, and then back outside. I was breathing, but I felt like I could not breathe at all. I felt panicked, like I was about to hyperventilate. I wanted to tear the mask off and undress. It was all I could think about. The mask rattled against my cheeks, warning me I was low on air. The rattle and flashing LED increased as the tank's air supply continued to decrease. If I had been inside a burning building, this warning told me it was time to get out. After seventeen minutes, I ran out of air and I was gasping. The mask fogged and sucked tighter and tighter to my face.

Done, I took the mask off, and shook off the gloves. I removed every piece of gear as if acid was eating through it and would soon devour my flesh. My clothing under the turnout gear was drenched in sweat. I wanted to throw up, but I took slim satisfaction knowing I'd done it. I'd completed the training drill.

I quit the department. There was no way I'd be of use to anyone in an emergency situation if my claustrophobia struck. The worst, and most embarrassing thing about it all had been going back to work after quitting. While the idea of volunteering and being productive had earned me nothing but support from my peers at 9-1-1, I was certain I'd look weak and lazy when I returned. No one ever said the latter. On some though, I saw it in their eyes.

"Chase, we got movement ahead from the trees," Dave said.

Shit. That brought me out of my daydream. "What do you see?"

"Too dark, but we saw something. Not far. Get back in here."

The attempt to free Palmeri from under the plane was futile. Nothing under here was loose. I'd wiggled and jiggled anything and everything I could get my hands onto, and nothing. If something was out there, I was a sitting duck. The top half of my body was wedged inside this damned heap of now-twisted metal.

"Chase?"

"I'm coming," I said. I wanted to slide back out carefully. I had no idea how bad the cut on my side was. It still bled, that much I knew. I could feel the stickiness of it. I tried to kneel as I raised my arms up and lowered myself out of the hole.

"Chase--there is something out there. In the bushes by the road, maybe. I'm coming out there."

"No! No. I'm almost out. Watch the door."

I freed myself from the frame and knelt with one hand on the pavement and sucked in a deep breath. It felt good to be out. Confined spaces sucked. I stood and stayed close to the frame and moved cautiously toward the door, my eyes trying to look everywhere at once. I wished I could use the powerful flashlight. I think the last thing I'd want to see is a herd of zombies right in front of me. To not know would be best, or better, anyway.

Dave was at the opened door, held out a hand and hoisted me into the plane. "You're hurt," he said.

"Dad?"

I put a hand up. I probably needed stitches, but this was not the time to worry anyone. "I'm okay, guys. I cut my side. It's just a cut."

"We can't defend the plane, not with that," Dave motioned toward the gaping hole where a wing was once affixed.

"Get ready to move. Make sure we bring anything that looks useful," I said to Allison and Charlene. "Dave, come with me."

We went to the cockpit.

"There are things out there. I don't think they're people. The movement is all sluggish," Palmeri said. "They either can't hear us, or the plane is confusing them. It reminds me of monkeys. Staying close to the trees, checking it out."

"They're zombies," Dave said.

"She's right. I've noticed things like this, too. When I killed my ex-wife, she'd been in a bedroom looking at a picture of the kids. If she wasn't remembering, then she was remorse*ful*. It was creepy to see."

"She was a--one of those things?" Palmeri said.

I nodded. "And when we were at the internment camp, I saw one of them step on the corpse of another trying to get closer to the top of the fence. It looked down at the corpse, looked up at the top of the fence, and then used that body like a stepstool. I shit you not. I'd also used a belt to lock the gate. Buckled it, but those bastards unbuckled that belt and got out. They figured out what the problem was and they solved it."

"You never said anything earlier," Dave said.

"We haven't exactly had time."

"That's bullshit," Palmeri said. "You should have told us."

"What difference does it make? Even now, the things are out there in the woods and are being cautious. They're not coming right out and attacking. What are you going to do differently? Nothing." I didn't want to yell. "Now, we have to get you the fuck out of that seat."

Palmeri's face paled. I don't think it had anything at all to do with my raising my voice. "Chase, if you lift me there's a pretty good chance I'm going to bleed-out."

"If you stay here, there's a better chance that our smart zombies out there will bite you. Not much choice in the matter," I said.

The cockpit was unbelievably small. The shaft protruded a good seven inches out of Palmeri's thigh. We would need to lift her straight up and off the shaft. I was not sure how we could do that. There was little to no room to work with.

"I have to pull Erway out," I said. I reached over and unfastened her seatbelt. I had to stay hunched over, my head banging into the instrument panel on the top ceiling part of the pit. I pushed Erway forward so I could better grasp her arm and shoulder, and then I heaved, lifted, and pulled all at once. Her thighs smacked against the thrusters in the center between the pilot and co-pilot seats as I kept stepping back. Dave grabbed her waist and then legs, helping me move and gently set the paramedic down.

"We're going to have to do this quickly, because our monkeys are getting more adventurous," Palmeri said.

I looked at Dave. "Get ready to run."

"What about . . .?" He pointed toward the cockpit.

"I'm going to get her out and then we're running."

"I'll help."

"We can't both fit up there."

"I'm helping," he said.

CHAPTER ELEVEN

I had one foot on the floor, a knee in the co-pilot seat and was bent forward to keep from banging my head on the toggles and switches on the above instrument panel. I did my best *not* to think about Erway dying in this spot. It wasn't working. It wasn't that I felt her ghost, but I had chills. "You're going to have to help as much as possible," I said.

Palmeri's face was covered in a sheen of sweat. She nodded. "I'll try."

"It's going to hurt, probably a lot." I smiled, as if I were joking. She didn't. I placed one hand over her thigh, the other under the thigh by where her knee bent. Dave stood, holding Palmeri's outstretched arm and under her shoulder. "On three," I said.

The count was silent. The three of us head nodded at each other. *One. Two. Three...*

Palmeri let out a scream and I cringed. She must have known better because she bit her lip. Sweat poured profusely from her brow. The shaft and wound made a horrible sucking sound as her thigh rode up the length of metal.

The angle I was at was more than awkward. We needed to lift her at least another three inches to clear the shaft. It wasn't happening easily.

"Chase," Dave said.

I knew what he was going to say. He dropped to his knees. Now crying silent sobs, Palmeri placed her arm on his back and pushed, as he set his arms under her ass and lifted. I heaved, trying to keep the leg as straight as possible. Blood bubbled up from the wound. I thought I could smell it; coppery and metallic. The sight of it was a bad sign. Palmeri looked at me, eyes wide.

"It's nothing," I said.

"Stop," she said. "Set me down."

"We're not putting you down," Dave said. With a final grunt, he pushed and she rose, her thigh clearing the top of the shaft, and she was freed.

Moving her out of the pilot seat, and out of the cockpit, with me stepping onto and over the co-pilot seat and center console, we set her down. I looked up. Allison and Charlene were watching us. They had their gear gathered by the door, ready to run.

"I need something to tie off the thigh," I said, and moved beside Palmeri. She took my hand and squeezed it hard. "We're going to stop the bleeding and then hobble our asses to somewhere safe."

"Just go," she said.

Charlene pulled the knife from the sheath on her hip and tore at the tarp she had bundled up. She cut a long piece out of it and gave it to me. "I'm going to need a stick or something," I said.

Everyone searched the plane as I wrapped the piece of tarp around her thigh and began twisting it tighter and tighter in place. We were going to have to make a tourniquet. No EMS would be responding, and I didn't know how else to stop the bleeding.

She was bleeding a lot. It wasn't spurting, but it was pouring and pooling around my knees. "A stick!" I said.

I removed my knife. I fit it between the ends of the tarp and used it to twist the tourniquet as tight as possible. I held it in place. If I removed my hand from the knife, the pressure would loosen and the blood would continue to flow from her. For now, it seemed to have stopped. "We're going to get you out of here."

Palmeri's lips mostly trembled, as if tremendous amounts of strength was needed to attempt a smile. "This isn't going to work. If there are fast ones out there, and there are bound to be fast ones, I am either going to slow you down, or risk getting all of us caught. I won't have that on my head, I won't."

"We're not leaving you," I said.

"Dad," Charlene said.

I looked up. She waved me over. She and Allison were squatting, looking out the hole in the side of the plane. "Hold this," I said, and placed Palmeri's hand on my knife. "We're not done talking about this, you got it?"

She nodded. "Got it."

I stood up and Dave and I walked toward my daughter. "What is it?"

"Looks like a building over there just off the road. It doesn't look that far. I think we can make it."

Allison was nodding. "Looks like a school."

A school would mean a nurse's office, cafeteria and bathrooms. "I like it. Dave?"

"Best plan we've got. You and I can carry Palmeri. Allison and Charlene can cover us," he said.

"If the doors are locked?" Charlene said.

"Worry about that when we get there," I said, and shrugged. "Let's leave those things here. Just take our weapons. If it is a school, we'll have more supplies, better supplies in there." "We really only found the tarp."

"Perfect, leave it," I said. "Okay, let's get Palmeri."

I went back to her. She'd removed the knife, the makeshift bandage, and lost so much blood that the color had drained from her face and lips. She looked pasty white, and blue. Again, she tried to smile. "I'm sorry," she said, and held out her hand.

We laced fingers. "What were you thinking?"

"You guys have to get out of here, get out of this plane," she said, and then her body spasmed with a series shivers.

I re-wrapped the bandage around her thigh.

Palmeri put a hand on mine, and shook her head. "It's too...it's too..."

There was nothing else. Her eyes and mouth stayed open. Vacantly, she stared at me. More ghosts to haunt my nightmares. I lowered my head and rested my forehead against her hand, our fingers still laced together.

"Chase," Dave said. "Chase."

I pulled away, released her hand and retrieved my knife. "Okay, we're moving. Ready?"

# # #

I stepped off the plane first and looked left and right, holding my sword in both hands. Those things might have been holed up in the woods, but with Palmeri's scream, hell, with the plane crashing out of the sky, they had to be beyond curious and ready to investigate. I didn't see anything. Not a single zombie anywhere. Once I felt confident there wasn't any immediate danger, I turned and held out a hand and assisted my girlfriend and daughter. Next, and lastly, I helped Dave out of the plane. I wasn't sure if he would accept my hand, but he did. He took it.

"What have we got?" Allison stood beside me, her sidearm gripped tightly in hands with arms extended. "The woods are to the left and behind us, and the school, if that's what it is, is to the right, that way."

I saw two signs in the bit of moonlight that challenged the surrounding darkness. We had landed on RT 68, New Castle Rd. "It's Butler High School," I said. "That was a good call, Charlene."

We stayed low. "Move together," Dave said.
"You take point," I said. "I'll bring up the back end. Let's stay close, clustered, okay?"

Dave nodded.

"Freeze! Hands up."

I had to look around. I wasn't sure where the voice came from, but I froze. "Stop everyone," I said, hoping it came out in a whisper. "Dave? You see--"

"No talking!"

"We are no danger to anyone here. We're just making our way through," I said. It wasn't zombies in the woods. It was people. Fucking people. We'd rushed to free Palmeri exposing whatever main artery had been severed and she'd bled to death when maybe we didn't have to.

"All four of you are armed like you're dangerous!"

"They are not getting our weapons." Despite the fading light, I saw Dave grind his teeth.

"I said no talking!"

"Why don't you show yourselves," I said, still unable to pinpoint where the voice came from. I didn't think it was to the left or the right, but neither did it seem to be from in front of us, either. "I'm telling you, we do not want any problems. To be honest, food, water, maybe bathrooms is what we're looking for and then we are on our way. That's it. That's all we want."

"And what will you do to get food and water?"

"What will we do? We'll look for it. We'll keep moving until we come across it," I said.

"You'll keep moving."

"That's what I said." I think it came from the woods, now to our right, where we thought the zombies had been. It was no wonder they hadn't just attacked us when we crash landed, or when I was underneath the plane trying to free Palmeri. It wasn't like the zombies I'd witnessed learning, they weren't being cautious. It hadn't been zombies at all.

"You'll keep moving now."

I lowered my head. "Look, man, we're hungry, tired and we need water. You go your way, we'll go ours."

"It's not going to work like that. You're going to start walking now, walking west on this road, and we're going to watch you until we can't see you anymore, or until we get tired of following you. Understand?"

We're going to watch you? That is what he said.

"Chase?" It was Dave.

There was no need for a pissing match. I had no idea how many "we" equaled, but I knew my "we" was just the four of us, and one of my four was fourteen years old. I gave some vigorous head nods, knowing full well they could see us. I'd wager some rifles held us in crosshairs. That wasn't a farfetched assumption. "Fine. You want us to just keep walking, we'll just keep walking. Appreciate the Pennsylvania hospitality. I'll be sure to tell friends and family to stop by if they're ever in your back-ass, redneck part of the woods."

"Daddy!" Charlene hushed me. She was right. There was no need to tempt this group of strangers. We knew nothing about them. Getting to walk was better than getting killed.

"Sorry," I said, whispering. "I'll take point. Stay close."

I led them. We took several steps away from the plane. The progress was slow. I wasn't about to start running. Part of me hoped to catch sight of them, or of at least one person watching us. I wasn't going to do anything about it if I saw them, but I just wanted to see them. I didn't like the bully-tactics, however, I did understand them. What was becoming par for the course was protect your own. The guy talking to me could be some guy just like me, with a girlfriend and kids and some friends, and he didn't know us, didn't trust us. He didn't have a reason to trust us. I think given the same set of circumstances--some plane falls out of the sky during a zombie apocalypse, and a small band of heavily armed people emerge--I'd send them walking, too. I know I would.

"How far we going to walk?" Dave said.

"Until we're sure they're not following us," I said.

"And then what?"

"We find a place to hole up for the night. And in the morning, we keep walking," I said.

"Somewhere with food and water," Charlene said.

"Ideally," I said.

That was when the screaming started; screaming and shots fired.

CHAPTER TWELVE

"They're in trouble," Allison said. It was a needless statement. We all knew it. Maybe because we kept walking, she felt like it needed to be said.

"We're not stopping." I looked back, toward the sound of gunshots, toward the sound of screaming. The moon was out. I still could not see a thing beyond a few yards. Not even shadows. It was just darkness from where we had come. "The things must have come out of the woods. Was more than just those people back there."

"We're not going to help them?" Allison said. She spoke in a whisper. I heard the tug in her words. She wanted us to stop.

"They weren't going to help us," Charlene said. "They kicked us out, made us leave."

They weren't going to help us.

She was right, of course. We just wanted somewhere safe to rest. Food. Something to drink. They weren't going to help us. "Wait," I said.

"What?" Dave said.

I had to think about the future. There was no guarantee one way or the other about anything, except I knew if we were to survive as a civilization, as fucking humans, even if they weren't going to help us… Did we want to be like that? Did we…did I want my daughter to be like them, pushing people away, not afraid to help, but unwilling to do so?

She'd be safer, yes, but she'd be alone. I wasn't always going to be here; wasn't always going to be around. It was parenting. My job wasn't done. She was tough. She'd proved as much. She could handle weapons, and heartache and adaption. Where was the compassion and empathy going to come from, if not from me?

God, my thoughts made me nauseated. Mushy, and fucking flowery, but I was right. I knew I was. I knew we needed to do this. We had to make a difference. "We're going back."

"What?" Charlene said.

"What if that was us. What if we were the ones back there fighting off those things. Wouldn't we want, wouldn't we pray for help?"

"We might," Charlene said. "But we wouldn't expect it from a group of people we'd just chased off, that we'd just threatened."

"Exactly. That's why we're doing it, going back."

Allison pursed her lips and nodded.

"Dave?" I said.

"I'm with you. Have been since the beginning. If I wasn't, I'd just tell you to go fuck yourself."

I laughed. "I know that you would."

We weren't going to be heroes about it, though. I told everyone, as always, to stay close. We went in packed tight and staying in the center of the road. Each of us had weapons drawn. Dave and Allison had their side arms out, Charlene and I had our swords.

We'd walked further than I'd thought. I was just starting to make out the shape of the airplane in the road. I saw the white flash of rifles being fired off toward the right, toward the high school, and pointed. We didn't want to get caught in crossfire, or accidentally mistaken for zombies. That really hadn't been something I'd thought of, not until now, anyway.

And then I saw them. Just beyond the plane, on the grass by the front of the school. The band that had forced us away was huddled together, not unlike us. They were taking shots down the road, east.

"We're here to help," I said, loudly. I wanted them to know they had actual people behind them, and that we were not sneaking up on them.

A man spun around, rifle aimed at us. "Who's here to help?"

"Gene!" It was a woman.

Gene turned back to face the zombies and fired.

"They're getting closer," a man said. "There might be too many of them!"

"There are," a different woman said.

Dave ran forward, knelt beside the group and fired off six shots. I had no idea how he'd improved his aim in days, but he had. Four of the six shots were head shots, and those hit, fell and stayed down.

Allison joined them, firing round after round.

I looked at Charlene. I knew she knew what I was thinking. The guns were great, especially for hitting targets further away. All the ammo being spent had to force people to realize that once it was gone, it was gone. You might carry extra bullets or magazines, but how long would they last? A few extra days? Weeks? And you might find more, but the question didn't change. How long until your guns were useless? The answer was simple, if vague. Eventually.

A zombie got close, on the right, and Charlene walked toward it. She held her sword in both hands, blade pointed at the moonlit sky. She resembled a ballplayer in the batter's box. I almost yelled for her to stop, to let me handle it, but was startled when Dave shouted my name.

Two creatures were close to me, so close, so silent that Dave couldn't get off a shot. The tip of my blade had been pointing at the grass. I brought sword up and swung right to left in a single fluid motion. Passing through an arm and ribs and the other arm did little to detract from the impact of the swing. I felt the impact in my hands. The sharpness of the blade and the power behind the swing cut the first and closest in two. The top half of the body slid off from the lower, it made a *thwash* sound as it hit cold grass. The arm stumps raised and reached, and its head still had the sense to gnash teeth as if it were moments from a meal, instead of seconds from me driving the blade through its temple with a fisted plunge.

I heard a gunshot and thought I heard a single bullet whiz by my head. Allison's target had been the second zombie. Like Dave, she'd improved. The female monster collapsed, thick black blood oozing from an entry wound above the decaying left eyeball.

I'd missed Charlene's kill. The creature's head was chunked open like a pie wedge had been cut from the skull. She had blood spray on her clothing and skin.

"Is there someplace safe we can run to?" I said.

"The school, we should get back inside the school," Gene said. He waved at everyone.

We followed close behind Gene and his group. I stayed in back and kept checking over my shoulder. Seemed like mostly slow moving zombies, thankfully. Didn't make them any less dangerous. In large numbers, it's easy to get overwhelmed, and that was where having swords and machetes sucked. It was one thing to fight off a handful of creatures with steel, but the idea of killing an circling mass and surviving with just a sword was unlikely.

Our entire group moved like a snake, one behind the other, not toward the school's front entrance, but around to the side of the building. We didn't stop there either. There were no doors, but many of the windows were boarded up, suggesting this might be the group's safe haven. I did not see any doorway into the school though.

We reached, not the back, but another corner of the high school building, I knew we'd put some considerable distance between us and the zombies. So much so, I'd stopped checking over my shoulder every other second. By the three large green dumpsters, I saw a door.

Gene jingled a set of keys. It was a big ring, one a janitor might carry. The woman who always seemed by his side urged him on with her hands going up and down. "Hurry, Gene. Hurry, please."

"Gene," one of the other guys said and kept looking from Gene to the corner. If zombies rounded it, we'd be trapped in this nook, this alcove area.

I took a quick inventory. There were seven of them; three men and four women. We didn't have long. The zombies after us might be moving slowly, but they were walking toward us. "Gene," I said.

Gene inserted a key. I heard the lock springs click, disengage.

He pulled open the door. "Inside, everyone!" Again, he waved us forward with a hand, and through the threshold into the school before closing and locking the door behind us.

"Get them to the cafeteria," Gene said. "Hurry."

We followed them down dark hallways lit only by a red glow from generator powered electricity. We made a series of lefts and rights. The group we followed didn't move slowly, or cautiously. My guess was that the school was secure, and had already been checked for the creatures. That, or we were going about this race for the cafeteria all wrong and walking decay could be waiting for us behind every corner.

It took mere minutes, two tops, before we reached the cafeteria. The outside walls were made of glass or Plexiglas so anyone in the hallway could see who was inside the cafeteria. We entered between standing open double doors. The walls *inside* looked as if they had been painted by student artists. Clouds with planes, rainbows, a sun, and a pot of gold. The back wall, however, was an American flag.

I could not help but think about the mess we'd gotten ourselves into with the Terrigino Brothers. We'd looked to them for help. They looked at our women as a way of re-populating the planet.

Just where the fuck were we?

CHAPTER THIRTEEN

Butler County High School -- 2321 hours

"Sit," Gene said. No one moved. We'd fought a common enemy, but that didn't make us friends. My group and I had returned to help after hearing gunshots and screaming, but the tension between the twelve of us was thick, almost visible. "Sit, please!"

There were eight chairs per round table, and more than twenty tables in all. The room was split in half. Straight ahead were two separate doors. Looked like one you entered to get your food, and the other you exited after paying. From here, I could see the white cash register.

The eerie red glow from mounted floodlights set a mood.

I wasn't a man of words. If I had to name it, I'd label it: Distrust.

I sat at a table to the left of Gene. Allison, Charlene and Dave followed suit. We sat more side-by-side, despite the shape of the table. Gene nodded toward us, a clear sign of appreciation. Then he turned and faced his people, and with his hand, waved at the table next to us.

The group sat, but ignored the table next to us and instead opted for the opposite side of the aisle between the two rows. Gene shook his head and clapped his hands in surrender against his thighs. "Whatever. Fine. Sit where you'd like."

"We need food," I said.

"We'll get to that," Gene said. "We have food. Water. You--you're bleeding. . ."

A guy at the other table jumped up, pointed a handgun at me.

Dave did the same, leveling his weapon at the man.

"He bit?" the guy said. He was big, dressed in black and yellow, hometown Pittsburgh Steeler get-up. Nothing like a die-hard of any sport. Always a little off their rocker, if you ask me.

"I don't know, Andy. Who had time to ask?" Gene said. "Sir, were you bit by one of...one of those things out there?"

I shook my head. Wasn't an easy way to explain it. "Cut myself in the plane."

"The plane?" Andy said. "Lift your shirt. I want to see. I don't wanna see any bite marks. I see bite marks, we've got a problem."

"He doesn't have to do shit." Dave pulled back the hammer on his gun.

"If you guys want food, a place to rest, I'm afraid he does," Gene said. Sounded like a diplomat.

I put my hand up to Dave to stop him. "They're right. Lower the gun."

I unzipped my vest, and lifted the flannel shirt up. The cloth material had dried to the wound. "If I pull, I'm going to start the bleeding again," I said.

Gene took a step closer. "Melissa, please go fill a pitcher with warm water. Grab some napkins, too. Sir, why don't you lie down on the table? Let me have a look."

"You a doctor?" I said, missing Erway, more than just *our* token paramedic.

"I'm the school janitor, but I have training," he said.

"EMT? Paramedic? You ride with an ambulance?" Charlene said.

"Internet."

I laughed. Thought Gene might, too. He didn't. "Wait, what? You're serious?"

"Gene is a survival nut. One of those guys they might do a TV show on. You know, turned his house into a bomb shelter, can live off the land, that kind of thing," Andy said.

"All from the internet?" I said. I hoped the sarcasm wasn't

dripping. "Like what? One of those preppers?"

"We pull that shirt off the cut, you're right, gonna hurt."

Melissa, with long dark hair, returned. She didn't say anything but instead poured the water onto my chest. It wasn't warm, as suggested. I cringed, and my muscles tightened as it soaked the flannel before I slowly lifted it off my skin.

"That's nasty," one of the other women said. "He's going to need stitches. A lot. You say you got that from the plane crash?"

"More or less," I said. I looked for Andy and locked eyes. "But I wasn't bitten."

"I'm convinced," Gene said. "Kia, you want to run and grab the sewing kit. It's right in the desk drawer in the nurse's office."

"I can do that." Kia was taller than me, although I was only 5'8". She had dark, black skin, big brown eyes and a very infectious smile. She appeared both confident and tough. I liked that. Strong and tough were two qualities that demanded admiration. For some reason, although, she hadn't proven a thing, right now she had mine.

"While we wait, why don't we introduce ourselves?" Gene said.

I closed my eyes. Ice breaking games and shit wasn't what I was in the mood for. I wanted a shower. Late dinner. Cold beer. And, God, how long has it been since I've had a cigarette? Far too long. I wasn't just *jonesing*, I felt itchy all over from withdrawal symptoms.

"My name is Gene," he said. "This is my wife, Melissa."

"Gene. Melissa. Hi. I'm Chase. As much as I want to do this, go around the table and discuss life. I think we need to make sure this place is safe, that those things can't get in here. That they aren't already in here making their way towards the cafeteria," I said.

"Chase. I like that name. It's different," Gene said.

"I do, too," Melissa said.

I hope I closed my eyes before I rolled them again. To say mental red flags were raised might have been an understatement. "Guys? Gene, I'm not kidding around."

"Oh, we're safe. Very safe. We cleared this place out. Wasn't easy. Lost a lot of good people. Damned good people. It was worth the fight though, or so it seemed. All the windows are boarded, doors locked. Generator is running low so we don't consume all of our resources. We've got a lot of dry food, and best of all, running water. There's a weight room, Olympic sized swimming pool…"

"Gene. Gene. Can I stop you there?" I said, and sat up. I winced and Allison grabbed my arm, assisting. We didn't want to hear shit about a weight room and swimming pool. Was this guy out of his mind? I could not imagine going for a dip any time soon. I saw Charlene out of the corner of my eye. She was watching *them*, her hand on the hilt of her sword. "We're thirsty, I mean, very thirsty."

Gene nodded and lowered his head. "Forgive me. I'm just, well…after the way we treated you. It wasn't anything personal. I'll be the first to admit I was surprised when you returned to help us. Because I'll be honest, if the situations were reversed, I am not so positive we'd have come back. I'm sorry to admit that. I hate that it is what it is. But, well, I guess it is what it is, you know? Megan, Michelle, you mind getting them some nice glasses of water, please?"

"I'll help."

"Thank you, Robert," Gene said.

Melissa, Megan, Michelle. Great. Kia, Andy, Gene and Robert. I sucked at names. "We appreciate it."

"I can help, too," Allison said.

"That's not necessary," Gene said.

"No. I want to," she said, and gave me a little wink. I knew what she thought. I had the same idea. I wanted to drink and enjoy a nice glass of water, not worry something might have been slipped into it. Allison would ensure that at least nothing had been tampered with.

She followed them.

Kia returned, and held a small plastic box. "I have it."

"We don't have anything for the pain, I'm afraid," Gene said. "This wound looks like it's going to take a bit of sewing. It is probably going to hurt a good deal, but we can repair you. I can't stress how important it is going to be for you to keep it clean, though. Without any antibiotics, you washing this area good is about all you can do to fight the chances of infection."

"I understand," I said. "You've done this before?"

He shrugged, cocked his head to the side. "Sort of. YouTube."

I stared at him.

"I'm fucking with ya," Gene said. He laughed. Slapped a hand against his thigh, against Kia's back. "I've stitched a few times. Like five. It's not so tough. Just that…that pushing the needle through someone's skin is awkward. It's actually pretty weird."

CHAPTER FOURTEEN

I tried to ignore the hooked needle Gene threaded. As he used a lighter to sterilize the tip, Kia knelt beside me. I smiled or tried to. I took quick shallow breaths in anticipation of the discomfort headed my way.

"I was in my house when all of this started to happen," she said. Talking to me was meant as a distraction. I think I preferred being stitched in silence, but wasn't in a position to argue the point. "My husband and I. We'd had dinner, and were watching television when we heard sirens outside. There were police cars and fire trucks. About seven houses down, the place was going up in flames. Everyone was outside watching. You know how neighbors are. We weren't any different. Thing was, the bizarre thing was, I didn't recognize a lot of the people. They were everywhere. They came out of everywhere."

I felt like a human quilt as Gene slipped the needle through my skin. The area was raw, and it felt more like a dagger being jammed into my side. "There we go," he said.

"Look at me," Kia said, and took my hand. I squeezed it tighter than expected when Gene tugged on the thread and pulled it through before dipping the needle into the next part of flesh. "The people were drawn to the flames it seemed. They reminded me of like, I don't know, fireflies or something. I noticed that some of them just didn't look right. They had bite marks, and peeled back skin. They looked like they were rotting. Their skin was purplish, and pasty, and that was when they started attacking the firefighters. Just, they just, went right at them. Tackled them. The fire hose dropped. It went wild. It sprayed everywhere with just tremendous force. It pushed back a lot of the...of those things," she said.

"They don't seem to like water," I said.

Gene nodded. "We've noticed. Too bad we're going into winter and not spring."

"The police had their weapons drawn, but they hesitated. I mean, the idea of shooting people at the fire, it was all surreal, even to the officers on scene there, I guess. And my husband, he tried to help. He went after the fallen firemen, and tried to get those things off of them. He did, too. He got them off, but the guy he'd saved was apparently beyond help. And then they were on him. They got my husband and I just stood there, watching. They bit him and kept biting him, and..."

I pursed my lips as she cried. I didn't have comforting words. There weren't really any to share. "How did you get away?"

The needle hurt like a motherfucker. I couldn't watch the work Gene did. While I didn't want Kia's distraction, I found it worked. Only I didn't like seeing her this upset.

"Got away just barely. When the police started shooting, when they finally realized something was very wrong and opened fire on these things, on the zombies surrounding us--one of them yelled for me to run, to get out of there. I didn't want to, you know. I wanted to help my husband. I didn't go to him. I don't think he was dead. But I ran. I left him. I..."

Now she squeezed my hand. Her shoulders shook in time with her sobbing. "It couldn't have been easy," I said. It was the best I could offer.

She tried to smile; fought to regain composure. "It wasn't. It hasn't been for any of us. And I'm sure it wasn't for anyone in your group, either."

I thought of Cash. I missed him. My heart felt so empty. "No. It hasn't been."

"We have water," Allison said. She stood beside Kia and me, looking back and forth at us. "You guys okay?"

"Just taking his mind off Gene's needlework."

"It helped," I said. "Thank you."

# # #

"So they learn?" Kia said.

We sat at two tables in the cafeteria. There was indeed a lot of food. We'd prepared a meal of grilled cheese sandwiches and tater-tots. We used napkins and kept the food on trays. The tots were crisp and golden brown, and actually, so were the sandwiches. The flavor was amazing, even brought back childhood memories of similar lunches in similar cafeterias when I had been a teen.

"It's what I've come to learn," I said, after I'd explained my reasoning behind my assumption. I picked up a tot and drove it through a pond of ketchup and popped it into my mouth. As I wiped my fingers on a napkin, I said, "But I don't know what that means."

"Could mean a number of things," Melissa said. She held a triangle wedge of her sandwich in one hand and a couple of tots on the tines of her plastic fork in the other. "I was thinking about this earlier. What if the vaccinations infected people, but wear off after a certain period of time? You know almost like it is a virus *inside* the vaccination. So the things out there," she pointed at a wall with the sandwich wedge, "are, essentially, you know, sick."

"And then what?" Gene said. "They become normal, human, again? Slowly, but eventually, they get better."

"I haven't seen any evidence of anyone getting better," I said. "Have you? Has anyone?"

No one nodded. Kind of killed the theory; made it useless without something to support the idea, other than mere wishful thinking.

"What about the people they bit, would they become human again, assuming it was a virus?" Allison said.

"I was thinking about why some are fast and some are slow," Megan said.

"Did you know Megan worked at The Living Dead Museum? It was created not long after George Romero's Night of the Living

Dead was filmed here. Right here in Butler County," Andy said.

Go figure. "Didn't know that."

"I do. I mean, I did. But what I was saying, what I was thinking was, the problem with a zombie is that it's dead, right? Reanimated flesh. Like what Frankenstein did with his monster. Brought a corpse to life, right?"

I thought it was rhetorical. When Megan didn't keep talking, I verbally agreed.

"Okay, so what happens to a body the longer it is dead?" she said.

"It decays," Charlene said, and dropped a tot back onto the paper plate on her tray.

"They do. That's right. But until they've been embalmed, there is all of that blood in them. And if blood isn't circulating, it's pooling. So if a dead zombie is chasing people, sure, at first it's fast. Eventually, that non-circulating blood is going to catch up with it. It's going to all sit in the thing's legs, right?"

"Right," I said.

"So, rigor mortis sets in. It's what makes them slower," she said. "But not just slower. It also means they are decaying. Ever wonder why you can stab them in the skull so easily? The bones are far more brittle. If they were healthy, there's no way I'd of been able to push a pocket knife, or even a hunting knife into the brain as easy as I have."

"That makes sense," Allison said. "I mean, that really makes a lot sense."

I nodded. "It does."

"But will they turn normal again?"

"I don't see how they can. They've died. They're dead. A better question might be, will they just eventually *stay* dead? Maybe the rigor mortis will stop them, and hunger and time will kill them, again, but for good," Andy said.

"I still don't understand why there aren't more survivors, or government action, or military involvement," Robert said. "I can't believe that you guys are the last of New York, and we're the last of Pennsylvania. That's just, I don't know, it seems impossible. Improbable. It all happened too fast to wipe out billions of people. Right? Or am I wrong? Am I missing something?"

"I agree," Michelle said. "So none of us got the flu shot. There's got to be more like us, people who are against it. Hell, the Appalachian area alone has got to be filled with people who didn't get the shot."

"There are probably a good percentage of people who didn't get the vaccination, but have they survived not getting bitten, too? How many planes have crashed, or trains derailed, or cruise ships sunk, or are floating aimlessly about on the oceans?" Gene said. "Forget the military, they get vaccinated for everything. Those shots probably killed our armed forces in days. Days."

And the military had a heads up, too. Just not a timely warning, unfortunately. I still suspected there were more military and political groups around, alive. It was a guess, of course, but seemed likely. "We have to assume pockets of people are all that is really left. Maybe pockets per county or town. Maybe only thousands of people per state, but not much more. I don't know," I said. "It is pretty mind blowing."

"So, I want to get this right," Gene said. "Your plan--what you guys want to do--is go to...Mexico? That's what you were saying, what you want? To cross the border because you think it will be safer *there*?"

I nodded. "It was my initial thought. Poorer countries didn't vaccinate their people. It's really all I was going with. I mean, this all came out of nowhere, I heard something on the radio..."

"Radio?" Gene said.

I shook my head. "That was days ago."

"But they'd still have zombies. Travelers, and people that *were* vaccinated, and then people who were bitten, too," Andy said. "That country isn't infection free. Or do you think it is?"

"They would have zombies, too. No doubt about it. But less than what's happened here in our country. And the wall we built to stop illegals from sneaking into the U.S., could now be used to keep infected Americans out. You've got the wall and the Rio Grande as a natural border. The things hate water," I said, but remembered the zombies aimlessly fell from the bridge over the Genesee River when we'd climbed onto the Coast Guard vessel. They didn't know enough to stay away from the river, despite not appreciating water. If they learned, however, it might not happen again.

"But why leave? Why risk crossing the country to get there, when we have everything we need here?" Andy said. He spread his arms wide and looked around the cafeteria.

"He's right," Gene said. "This place is great, but it isn't going to last. And hiding here, it's not going to rid the country of the millions of zombies. We'd just be biding time until we eventually ran out of supplies. And we would run out of supplies."

"We've got months' worth of food," Robert said.

"Exactly. Months. Then what? Then what do we do? Raids? Visit Costco and Sam's Club?" Gene shook his head. He reached for his wife's hand. "Chase has a point."

"But Mexico?" Megan said. She sounded doubtful. I shared that doubt, but wouldn't admit as much.

"Look," I said. "I wasn't telling you this to convince you to come with us. I was just telling you what we were thinking, explain what we'd been trying to do. That's all. Nothing else."

"You don't want us to go with you?" Gene furrowed his brow, narrowed his eyes.

"That's not what I mean. You want to come with us, that's fine. There's safety in numbers, and the work can be more evenly divided." Thought about clearing a building, or making that run through a Costco or Sam's. Everyone takes a turn, makes it better than just Dave and I always doing it.

"I know you weren't," Gene said. He looked at his wife, and she nodded. And he nodded back. "I've got a bus."

I closed my eyes. We didn't need a bus. We needed to travel a few thousand miles. We needed another plane. A bus was shit, a shit method of transportation.

"No," Melissa said. "It's not like you're thinking. It's a school bus."

I was glad my eyes were closed, because when I rolled them, no one saw. The fact that guy had a school bus really didn't make that bus any better, any more attractive an offer.

"Their right," Megan said. "I've seen it. It's a converted school bus perfectly designed for the apocalypse. If Romero had seen this thing, he'd of used it in one of his movies. It's even got one of those cattle scoopers on the front, you know -- like the ones you see on trains? They clear the tracks of animals and well, shit, anything, so the train can chug right along."

"Thing will destroy any cars blocking the road. Destroy them." Gene smiled, grinned really.

I looked at Allison, Charlene, and then at Dave.

Dave cocked his head to one side. "Let's see what this thing looks like."

"Good." Gene clapped his hands together. "Great."

"All right," I said. "So where is this monster masher of yours?" I asked.

"Well, see, that's where there's something of a problem," Gene said, his smile gone, his shoulders deflated. "It's not here."

"It's not here." I ground my teeth. Seemed like a school would be a perfect place for a school bus, but maybe not for a school bus with a cattle scoop.

"No. It's not."

I shouldn't have to ask the next obvious question. Gene didn't get the idea. It was his turn to talk, and reveal the location of his school bus. "Gene," I said. "Where is it?"

"Home."

"Home," I said.

"I was at work when everything started. I called Melissa, like I always did at the end of a day, you know, for a ride home."

"He doesn't have a license," Melissa said.

"I can drive. I drive fine. I know how to drive." Gene shook his head. "But, I lost it. Couple years back."

"He drives fine, sober," she said, and smiled at her husband, as if drunk driving was cute, and their little inside joke.

"And about the time she came to pick me up, hell was breaking lose all over town. Sirens blared. Cops running this way and that. We didn't know that it was zombies eating people. We had no idea what was really going on. When she got here, there was a ruckus going on over on the main road, fire engines and trucks had the road all blocked."

"Thought it was an accident, cars smashed all together, someone was trapped," Melissa said.

"So she came in," he said.

"And we never left. We followed all kinds of reports and

started locking the school down. Knew we had to make this place as safe as one of them underground bomb shelters. Our home is that way, too. End of times, and all that. People used to laugh at me, stocking supplies and weapons. I just always believed in being ready for anything."

"No one's laughing now," Melissa said, and placed an arm around her husband's waist.

No one is left alive to laugh, I wanted to say. "Gene. How far away do you live?"

"Across town," he said.

"I'm going with you," Charlene said.

"Honey, I didn't say I was going anywhere," I said.

"I'm going, too," Allison said.

I looked over at Dave, and he nodded. "You know I'm going. Don't need to hear me say it."

Gene nodded. "Well, kids, looks like we're taking us a field trip."

I needed to accept that Charlene was no longer a baby. I couldn't help recalling her days in kindergarten...

# # #

If it had just been the first day of school, I don't think I would have received a talking to. Instead, because I worked nights, I drove my daughter to school each morning. She had been in kindergarten and I didn't want her on a bus with kids in first, second and especially not third grade. I knew the innocence wouldn't last forever, and school was one of the first places to pick away at the sheltered wall her mother and I had built, but I was going to hold on to what I could for as long as possible.

We'd leave the house a little early, hit McDonald's for a couple of hash brown orders and juice, and get to school just ahead of the buses. We'd park in the visitor's lot, and wait for kids to get off the buses. She didn't like to be first and I didn't want to leave her alone in a classroom waiting for her friends, so hanging out until the buses arrived was fine with me. Then I'd carry her through the front doors.

She would talk my ear off the entire time. Usually the conversation revolved around cartoons, toys, or wanting to get a dog and why she'd be an amazing pet owner. How she'd take care of it, feed it, walk it, and wash it.

We'd smile and wave to staff as we entered the school.

On this particular day, Charlene's teacher met me at the door to the classroom. "Good morning, Mr. McKinney."

"Ms. Wingfield," I'd said.

"Can I have a word with you?"

I set Charlene down, gave her a kiss and a hug, and a little encouragement to go into her class. I waved to her as she finally crossed the threshold. "What's going on?" I said.

"I think it is time you stop carrying your daughter all over school."

I'd cocked my head to the side. "I'm sorry?"

"You daughter needs to walk to her class. At this point, I don't even think you should be walking her to class. You should say your goodbyes at the main door. She needs to begin developing some independence. You carrying her everywhere prohibits that from happening."

I had to search her face for a smile, certain it had been a joke. When there was no trace of anything humorous in the grim expression she wore, I almost lost it. I wanted to go off on her, ask her who the fuck she thought she was. Charlene wasn't always going to want me carrying her, so while she did, I sure as shit was going to. Was as easy as that.

"I've talked about this with your wife," she said.

Talking about it with my wife, did little--no, did shit--to influence my thoughts. I may have noticed when I spoke I was a little louder than I intended to get. "She carry her down to class, too?"

"No, Mr. McKinney, she does not."

"So she agrees with you?" I said. My hands were in my coat pockets. This was a good thing. I think if Ms. Wingfield saw my fingers roll into fists, the confrontation might have gone from bad to handcuffs fast. "Nah, I get it. I see what the two of you want. We'll see how it goes. Can't promise anything."

"She needs to learn, Mr. McKinney. The question is, are you carrying her to class each morning because she wants you to, or because you want to?"

I clucked my tongue. "You know what, Ms. Wingfield? You have a great day," I said, turned and walked away, back down the hall, toward the front-center of the school. Something needed punching. I just had to keep my cool until I was off school property.

By the time I reached my car, started it, and left the parking lot, I realized something I fought to admit.

Charlene needed to start walking to her classroom on her own. She did not need me carrying her to the door. The other kids in class would catch on, and make fun of her. She'd be remembered as the girl who had her daddy carrying her everywhere. Wasn't as terrible as the kid who was bound to shit his pants in class, but I didn't want my kid having to wear any labels.

# # #

"We've talked it over," Andy said. He stood with both his hands in front of his stomach. His fingers twirled around one another, and it seemed to take a large amount of control not to make eye contact with any of us.

"Talked what over?" Gene said, and took a step toward Andy.

Behind Andy were Megan, Michelle, Robert and Kia. Like Andy, not a one made eye contact. "We're not going."

"You don't have to," Melissa said. "The six of us are going to get the bus. You wait here."

"You guys can get some of the supplies together. Food in boxes, some of the medical stuff from the nurse's office. Meet us by the back bay door," Gene said.

"No." Andy shook his head from side to side. "You're not understanding me, us. You're not understanding us, we're not going with you on the bus. We don't want to go to Mexico," he said.

"No offense, Mr. McKinney," Robert said.

I held up my hands. "None taken."

"This is ridiculous," Gene said. "We've been together since the start. We're a family. I don't want us to split up. We need to stay together."

"Then stay with us," Kia said. "There's no reason to make a dangerous journey across town to pick up your bus, and then travel in it across the country just to cross a border. We have no proof Mexico is any better off than America. None."

"It was just something I heard," I said. I didn't feel defensive. These people had as valid a point, if not more, than my notion to cross into Mexico. "Only thing I keep thinking is that we need to keep moving. Staying in one place seems more dangerous, but that's just me. My thoughts. Mexico might be a million times worse off than the U.S. But it is something, you know? It's forcing us to do something."

Kia nodded. "I know and I respect your thinking, Chase; your decision. But it is *not* mine. I think it isn't that bad *here*. I'm staying at the school. Everything we need is here. Everything."

"Those supplies will run out," Melissa said.

"And I'll worry about that when it actually happens," Kia said. "We have the weapons that you had in the trunk of your car, and they'll--we can keep those weapons, Melissa, Gene? Can't we? You're not taking back all of those weapons?"

Everyone tensed. I saw hands tighten on rifles.

"They're yours. Everything here, it's yours. The bus is stocked. Prepped. We're not taking anything from you. I wouldn't do that. But, Andy, you're sure?" Gene said. "I am not comfortable leaving you. I'm really not."

Andy looked at the people behind him. They each cast a silent ballot with a slight nod. "We are," Andy said. "We're going to be okay."

"I don't like it," Gene said to Melissa, like they might be the only two in the room.

I understood the man's sense of feeling torn. "Gene, I think you guys should all talk. It's something we can discuss in the morning. I would never want to be the one to come between you and your family. The road is going to be very dangerous. At some point, we may have to leave your bus because of things blocking the way. This is not going to be an easy journey."

Not an easy and maybe not even a smart journey. This school wasn't so bad. It did have everything, and was close enough to surrounding woods that eventually hunting for food and other supplies might not be as deadly a task as it was currently. Maybe we all needed a night to think things over.

Gene nodded, wrapped an arm around his wife's shoulders. "You're a good man, Chase. And I agree with you. I do. It's very late. We should get some sleep, and in the morning, we can talk more. That sound alright?"

"Yes," I said. "Sounds fine."

"We've set the gym up like a mini-hotel. We pulled cots from the nurse's office, and gym mats to use as beds, and separated the gym with play props for borders," Melissa said, and smiled. "It's not so bad."

"I'm sure it's not," Allison said.

"Andy has sentry duty. Walks the halls, keeps an eye on things. It's a one level school, but it's spread out over a lot of land. We take turns doing this each night, using a rotation. Everyone has a turn," Gene said.

"Good system," Dave said. "I think I'll stay up with Andy. Get a feel for the place."

"That's not necessary," Melissa said.

"I want to, though. As long as it is alright with you, Andy?"

"I'd love the company."

Gene clapped his hands. "Sounds like a plan then."

CHAPTER FIFTEEN

Tuesday, November 3rd, 0725 hours

I woke up first. Allison, Charlene and I slept close to one another. The blue wrestling mat served well as a mattress. Walking around white tri-fold room dividers --more than likely from the nurse's office, I saw that the gymnasium was ours, and ours alone.

While the plan had been to talk before bed, we'd all been exhausted. As soon as we'd settled in, we'd fallen asleep. I'd slept well. Felt very rested, but no less conflicted.

Mexico.

I couldn't even remember what the radio broadcast announced, not exactly. That had been only an hour or so after Rochester had been severely hit with the outbreak, when Allison and I had been fleeing the 9-1-1 Center, and the journey to find and save my kids had first begun. The guy on the radio said people in poorer countries such as Mexico did not have the government funding to vaccinate their people. That the borders set up to keep illegal aliens out of the U.S. were now being used to keep infected Americans out of a less contaminated Mexico.

That had been about it. The extent of it.

It would be a no-brainer if we lived in Texas or anywhere near the Rio Grande. We didn't. We weren't anywhere near the south. We were thousands of miles away from the border. Was a bus with a cow scooper really going to be the salvation to deliver us to this massive wall?

It seemed doubtful. Unrealistic and disheartening.

The school really was a fortress. Possibly impregnable. The kitchen was huge. There were generators, and a room stocked with batteries to keep those generators running at least through the winter if incorporated discipline and restraint was used, so as to not drain all the juice in the first months or two.

If the Terrigino brothers' place hadn't burned to the ground, the cabin up along the St. Lawrence would have been ideal. But ideal because the area was isolated. Not as heavily populated as a Pennsylvania county. The cabin sat up high. Was more easily defendable. The problem had been the craziness of the brothers. Fighting a few zombies here and there was nothing compared to having to take those hunters out as well.

Winter was coming. That was surely a con. Generators or not. But was it really a negative, a con?

"Chase?" Allison said.

I moved back around the tri-fold. She was up on an elbow, hair disheveled. She looked beautiful. "Hey," I said, and spoke softly. Charlene was still asleep.

Allison stood up, stretched. If I didn't just see her wake up and *know* she was still groggy, I'd have sworn she was a zombie the way she walked; clumsy steps, ankle twisting, feet slapping onto the mat and then onto the gymnasium floor, thick with layers of polyurethane.

"What were you doing?" she said, wrapping her arms around my waist, and pressing her head to my chest.

I held her, my arms squeezing just as tight. It felt good, her warmth against me. I'd slept in the middle last night, between Charlene and her. It was not the same. I kissed her forehead. "Trying to figure out what's what, you know? If Mexico is right or wrong."

"I'm going wherever you go. So will Dave. You've got to know that by now."

"I know that. I do. That's the problem. I don't know where to go. I've made a million choices over the last few days. Not all of them good. Some of them, *no*, many of them put peoples' lives at risk. I am responsible for people dying."

"No, you're--"

"I am, Allison." I ground my teeth. "It's easy for people to look at what I've done and judge the mistakes I've made. I've tried though."

"Who's judging you?"

"I am." I pointed at my chest. "Me."

"Do you want to go to Mexico?" she said. "Do you think Mexico is the place we should head for? Chase?"

"I think we need to move south. Winter's coming. It's going to be cold here. Very, very cold."

Allison dropped her hands to her sides. "Can I say something?"

"You know you can." I reached for one of her hands.

"What if, like with rain, the snow annoys them? It's frozen rain, right? And eventually, that snow will melt. It will be rainy for the next several weeks before winter really hits. And then rainy after winter. We're not all that far from Rochester, really. The weather in western New York is practically the same here."

"Or worse."

"Okay. Worse. I'll give you that. We get a solid, what, two or two and half months of summer? But the rest of the time is either rain, or snow," she said. Maybe it was because I stayed silent that she became apprehensive. "It was just an idea. Just--it was just something I was thinking."

"No, Alley. No. I -- I get it. I see what you're saying. I do." I almost clapped a hand to my forehead. The obvious was that obvious, but I'd never seen it. Not like this, not until Allison pointed it out.

"Seriously? Because I was also thinking about what that woman… *Megan*…was saying. If rigor mortis is setting in, maybe the cold, the winter will wipe them out? I mean, unless they get smart enough to find shelter for the winter, you saw them, they just stumble about. A harsh Pennsylvania winter, Chase, it could kill them."

"And the ones that don't die, maybe the winter will at least slow them down, make them less threatening, easier to kill?"

"Just a thought," she said. "Like I said, just something I was thinking."

# # #

Locker room showers sprayed refreshing hot water. I was careful not to wet my new stitches. Allison helped redress the wound on my side afterward. We all looked battered and bruised. A few stitches up my side wasn't much of anything, considering there had been car accidents and gunfights. We'd battled zombies and survived inclement weather. There was the obvious, also, crash landing a plane just yesterday.

We even spent an hour using the football team's washer and dryer before meeting everyone back in the cafeteria for breakfast. Powdered scrambled eggs, sausage links and buttered toast. The best part was the coffee. I enjoyed two cups, despite the still nagging urge to smoke a cigarette. At this point, I was game for lighting up anything and just smoking that.

"Okay, Chase." Gene stood next to his wife, arms crossed over his chest. She had hands stuffed into the pockets of her jeans. "Melissa and I, we're with you. We're ready to go."

"Me, too," Megan said. Her face lit up with a smile. "And--I spent some time in the library last night. I found maps and compiled a list of directions and alternate directions in case we run into blocks we can't get around."

She held up folded maps and a notebook with a ton of words written on it. She wore a huge smile, and I knew she'd spent the night working on directions and not sleeping. If she'd have been wearing knee-high socks, a pleated skirt, and orange turtleneck sweater, I'd have sworn she'd pass for *Velma*.

Thankfully, Allison stood next to me, so I cleared my throat. I was an opening-mouth away from making myself look wishy-washy at best. "I'm not sure Mexico is the right place to go."

Andy sighed. I couldn't tell if he was relieved to hear the words said, or annoyed with me. Either way, he did not make eye contact, so I had no way of better assessing his sigh.

"Look," I said, and yes, felt immediately defensive. Dave and Charlene even looked at me, and the confusion they must have felt was apparent on their expressions. "I am not the leader. I don't have answers. I've said this from day one. I am just winging this--

all of it. I've made so many bad choices. I go left when right is obviously the better way. I just try to pick what I think is best at the time. I'm not going to lie; at the beginning, when all of this...exploded, I didn't really care about much else other than getting to my kids," I said, and stopped. I missed Cash. I failed him. My little boy. I lowered my head. I felt the heat in my face. My eyes were wet. "I don't know if Mexico is right. I just, I think it might be a mistake."

"So, what are you saying?" Megan said.

"I'm saying, I've done little else except focus on Mexico. But Mexico might not be the answer. It was just a means to keep me centered. It provided direction. A goal." Charlene moved closer to me, reached for my hand. She realized how difficult this was for me. I had no problem admitting when I was wrong. I struggled with admitting I didn't know what was right, or best. I laced my fingers with hers. "Alley and I were talking. She made some points that, I just couldn't argue against. And before any of us do anything, I think we should talk this out some more. All of us. Because right now, I've got to say that staying here in Pennsylvania, at this high school, at least for the winter might make the most sense. In the spring, I don't know what will come next. I don't. For now, I think we should talk. All of us."

Gene lowered his head.

"He has a point." Melissa tugged on her husband's arm.

"I want my bus." Gene looked up, looked over at me. "We should still go get my bus. It has more weapons. More supplies."

I was not sure he'd heard or comprehended anything I'd just said. I was not the leader. I was not in charge. If anything, he'd been the one in charge here. Why in the hell was he telling me he wanted his bus? I was not the one to grant or deny his request to go to retrieve his bus. It wasn't me. I wasn't that guy.

Allison said, "Gene, let's make a list of all of our provisions first."

"It's done," Michelle said. "We keep it in the kitchen. It's on a clipboard by the register. Every time we use something, we subtract it from the list."

"Good," I said. "That's excellent. Why don't you--"

The reserve lights mounted on the walls flickered, and then

went out.

"What just happened? What was that?" Charlene took a step back.

"The generator," Gene said. "It's a quirky piece of equipment. Thing gets used like once a year. Usually when we have a bad snowstorm. I can look at it."

"Where is it?"

"The generator's in the boiler room, back of the building," Dave said. "Saw it last night. Andy showed me around."

Gene nodded. "I can give you a tour of the mechanics of the place. I've shown Andy, who showed Dave and Megan. More people that know how this place works, the better. You never know who may need to know what, you know? Spread the knowledge."

I agreed. "Good call. Let's take a look."

"I'd like to see it, too," Charlene said, and kept a hand on the hilt of her long sword. She looked around, eyes taking in everything. I didn't like it either--lights just going off.

# # #

Charlene and I followed a step behind as we walked from the cafeteria and through the school hallways, the whole time my mind spinning. I'd made a grandiose speech back there. In telling everyone that I was not a leader, that I was not in charge, that I was not sure if Mexico was the right place to go or not, I still had my own reservations. If Gene all of a sudden said we were going to go to Arkansas, or Megan said New Jersey -- I'd say no. I wouldn't follow. I might not be a leader, I guess. Neither was I someone who followed. I didn't take direction well. Maybe that made me a dick. I'm sure it did. Part of me knew I still planned to call the shots. I couldn't change my nature. Not overnight, not even in the midst of...all of this. People were either with me, or they weren't. It was kind of that simple. The thing was, Allison was quite possibly right. She'd made sense this morning. I wonder how long she debated telling me any of it. There it was, again. I was a dick. At least I knew it.

"We keep the classroom doors closed, but not locked. Figure if anything gets in from one of the windows or something, we're hopefully going to hear the glass shatter. The closed door will be a good initial line of defense. We argued about locking them all, but then figured if those things are inside the school, a classroom might be a perfect place to hide. Can lock the doors from the inside, without a key." Gene made a motion with his hand, like he was turning a key. "And each classroom has fire windows. They swing open and are big enough to basically walk out of; ideal if getting out of the school is safer than staying inside it."

"You been with the school a while?" Charlene asked.

"Seems like I've always been here. Graduated from here. Went to college for business. Earned a degree and everything, but seemed like schools were kicking out business students by the bucket load. Finding a job, finding a good paying job that is, was impossible. Didn't matter I carried a solid GPA, either. Business graduates were a dime a dozen. So I came back home after a while. Moved back in with my folks, you know. That was one of the toughest things to do. After having the freedom of living on my own on campus, to go back to house rules and explaining where I'm going, who I'm going with and when I'd be home--about went insane. Within a few weeks, I knew I'd need to move out. Waited some tables at the Denny's, grabbed up a vacant studio, and when there was a janitorial opening at the high school, so I applied. Thought it would be temporary, a good job to hold me over until I could find something more in my field." Gene's walking slowed. He seemed almost lost in reflection.

"How did you and Melissa meet," Charlene said. My kid was smart. She'd sensed the funk the career conversation was causing, and knew to change the subject.

"That," Gene pointed a finger, "that is a great story. I mean, you've seen her. Look at me. You've got to be asking yourself, how'd this Joe Schmo wind up with a babe like that?"

We rounded a corner.

Gene stopped. Held up a hand. "Shh. Door's open. Shouldn't be."

"Mud," Charlene said.

It wasn't clearly footprints, but someone…or something, was wet and tracking mud around *inside* the school. "I'm guessing this wasn't how you left the mechanical room?"

"It was not," Gene said. "I'm going in. You guys have my back?"

Charlene already had her long sword drawn. I pulled mine from the scabbard. "We got you."

CHAPTER SIXTEEN

1002 hours

"Dad, I don't like this." Charlene held the hilt of her sword in both hands, the tip of the blade on the ground. She kept bouncing on the balls on her feet. She looked ready to swing that blade in any direction in an instant. Her eyes pivoted left and right and left.

"We need to warn the others. If they have weapons, we've got to be ready to kill them," Chase said.

"Weapons? You don't think it's those things?"

"Sneaking into the school, breaking into the mechanical room, and cutting the power from the generators?" I shook my head and almost snickered, but stopped. I thought about Charlene's mom and the photograph, and the zombies figuring out how to climb higher on a fence, and unfasten a belt. "No, dear, I do not think it's zombies. This is too well organized."

"I don't know which is better."

I knew. "It's people. Survivors. They're not friendly, though."

"How do you know that?"

"They didn't try to make contact. They…"

What they'd done instead was disorient and split the group. "Gene?"

"What is it?" Charlene raised her sword.

"Stay right here. I'm going after--"

The lights flickered on in the hallways. Gene must have

managed to restart the generators. Another flicker, two, and then they stayed on. From where we stood outside the Mechanical Room door, I could hear the motors of the generators whine as they geared up and sent out energy though the school.

"Gene?" I pushed the door open with the sword's blade, stood back, still cautious, still ready for anything. "Wait here, Char. Yell if you see anything."

There were green painted rails that followed down three cement stairs, and outlined and turned off this way and that down the small maze of different pathways. I knew nothing about machinery. There were dials, gauges, pipes. No idea. I wasn't even sure I would recognize a generator if I saw it. I assumed it looked like one giant car battery. A positive and negative lead...

"Gene?"

Something grunted. Groaned. I reset my grip on the hilt of my sword. I felt my breathing go quick, shallow. "Gene?"

"Chase?"

I spun, bringing the blade around fast, hard.

"Chase!"

I stopped, lost my balance doing so, stumbled forward and into a rail. I'd come a breadth away from chunking into Gene's ribs. "What the fuck!"

"What are you doing?"

"Fixing some of these wires. Trying to anyway. Going to have to get some electrical tape, do some splicing." He held them up. "They've been ripped out of electrical box, and the panel's a mess. I'm not sure I can fix it. The generators are up and running, for now anyway. Someone did this. I hate to think it's one of our people."

I wasn't about to play any finger pointing game. I knew it wasn't any of *my* people. He could be suspicious all he wanted. It was *his* people I did not know, *his* people I did not yet trust. "The mud, though, that suggested someone *just* came in from outside. Or, from somewhere wet and muddy. We should check the nearest doors. All the doors, actually. Did you check the whole school before? I mean, like the entire school top to bottom, left to right when you locked the place down initially?"

"I did. I do. We check everything regularly. Last night, they would have gone around checking classrooms, making sure windows were closed, locked. Doors, too. No one besides us is in here. Couldn't be." He bit his lower lip, pressed fists against his hips and looked around. I'd swear you could visibly see his confidence level descend.

"Char," I said, just before Gene and I emerged from the Mechanical Room and back into the hallway. I knew she was tense. I did not want to give her any reason to accidentally swing.

"Everything okay in there?"

I shook my head. "Someone messed with the wiring. Bad. We're going to check the doors around here. See if we can figure out how someone got in."

"Someone got in from out there?" Char shifted weight from foot to foot. I touched her shoulder. It was meant to mentally steady her. She shrugged the hand away. She was no longer fourteen. That age was gone. A simple number that meant absolutely nothing anymore.

"Place was locked up good," Gene said. "Andy and your man, Dave, they would have said something this morning."

Of course, they would have. I was not sure why the fresh mud tracks didn't alert Gene to the fact that whoever it was that had breached the school had just done so, or had so recently done so that they left a trail. "Let's get back to the others."

"I don't, ah, I need, I'm gonna need a weapon." Gene must have been comfortable with his notion that no one else could be inside the school. I hadn't even realized he'd walked the halls unarmed. I don't know that I'd ever go anywhere, ever again, without my steel.

I handed him a machete.

"These lights just went off, which means the person can't be that far." Gene held the blade by his side. His white knuckle grip revealed the panic he felt. I heard it in the way his voice cracked when he spoke.

There was only one set of prints that were too smeared to indicate whether they were coming or going. "We're going to check it out, Gene. Just not yet. Not now. They either knew we'd send a few to check the mechanical room for the problem, or knew that the lights going out would cause some chaos. Either way, what they wanted was an opportunity to strike. We've been divided. It's a ploy. They got us three away from the others. Let's not get surprised, okay? Char, you stay right behind me."

"Got it."

Not sure what I heard first. Someone, somewhere, screamed. There was also a raggedy mix of gunshots that echoed down the halls, bounced off metal lockers and square-tiled walls. The high school was under attack.

# # #

I led as we ran from the Mechanical Room toward the cafeteria. There was no way to prepare for horror. With the screams, and guns being fired, it was bound to be a mess.

"Whoa, wait!" I held out my arms as I skidded to a stop before rounding the last corner.

"What?" Gene said, and panted while bent forward as if trying to catch his breath.

Charlene answered the question. "We have no idea what's going down. We can't just, just -- barrel in there. Gotta take a peek, see what's what."

"Exactly," I said. "Exactly."

At the next corner, I laid down on my belly and inched forward. Peeking around the corner, I was not sure what I expected to see. Gunmen in black ski masks holding our families hostage. I suppose that is what a part of me thought might be waiting for us.

My imagination had failed me miserably. Kia, the woman who had comforted me yesterday while Gene stitched my side, was on her back. Someone straddled her waist. She had both hands planted on his head, forcing his mouth away from her throat.

"Shit." I pushed forward, legs kicked trying to get me up and propel me toward Kia.

"Dad!"

"It's zombies! It's motherfucking zombies!" I charged, sword raised. I wasn't sure I'd make it in time. Kia bucked, thrust her hips up, and twisted. It was enough to force the thing away from her neck. I swung my sword at its head. The force of the blow cut clean. The head rolled off the shoulders and landed with a splattering plop. Thick dark blood oozed from the corpse as Kia knocked it off of her and back-crawled away.

I held out my hand. "Are you okay?"

"The others are in the cafeteria!" Kia pulled herself up, looked around on the floor and found her 9 mm by the wall. The cafeteria was around the next corner. "I had them barricade the doors. I was on my way to warn all of you."

"How many? How many are we talking?" I led the four of us toward the next corner. The cafeteria would be roughly thirty yards from there. My sword was up, blade on my shoulder.

"A lot, seven, eight? I don't know. Ten?"

The lights in the hallway flickered and went out.

I looked back.

"The Mechanical Room. Want me to go fix it?" Gene started to turn around.

"No. Stay with us. We're done splitting up. We don't need the lights on. It's day time."

"They're doing this? Those things?" Kia said.

I nodded. "It seems that way."

"That's crazy. I mean, that's just impossible," she said.

"It's not," Charlene said. "They're either remembering, or they're developing survival skills. Whales hunt in packs and communicate attack plans as skilled as generals. Saw it on Discovery, or Animal Planet."

"She's right," Gene said, as if my daughter's comments needed confirmation. "Think I saw the same--"

"Shh," I said. "Listen, we need to round this corner and hit them fast. The school's no longer secure."

"We need my bus," Gene said.

"Not now," I said. "One thing at a time. Let's clear the hall outside the cafeteria and then figure out where to go after that."

"The gym," Gene said.

"Not the gym," Charlene said. "We need to get out of the school. We're trapped in here. This building is no longer safe."

She sounded as aggravated as I felt, and did nothing to hide it from her tone of voice.

"How much ammo you have?" I said.

Kia clapped a hand against her jeans. "Two more clips."

"Okay. Should be good. We'll do this together. On three. Ready? One. Two…"

CHAPTER SEVENTEEN

"…three!"

We rounded the corner and I counted eight zombies. They stood pressed against the glass wall of the cafeteria. Their flat palms left muddied prints on the glass. It baffled me how they'd staged and carried out such an elaborate attack. Somehow, the things figured out how to gain entry to a locked-down school, find the Mechanical Room and cut power to the generators, twice. It was like they knew that doing so would divide the group into two, and yet now they struggled with pulling on the door handles to enter the cafeteria.

If Charlene was correct, and I suspected she was, they had gained advanced animal-like survival instincts. This filled me with renewed fear, and meant we still didn't know our enemy, didn't have a clue what we were up against.

"Spread out some," I said. "But not too far."

"We've got this," Charlene said.

"Are you a good shot, Kia?" She shrugged. "With them that close, I can hit them."

"Head shots?" Charlene said.

"I can only do the best I can."

It might have been an honest answer. It wasn't a comforting one. "Okay. You are going to concentrate on taking them out. Head shots. Once you fire, the element of surprise is gone. If they're the fast ones, they are going to come at us without much time for reloading. Have your clips handy, okay?"

Kia immediately moved one clip to each pocket so that they protruded slightly. She checked her weapon. "We're good."

"Gene, Char, we're going to start toward them. Just a few feet out. Skirt the walls, okay? Char and me on this side. Gene, you've got that side." I wasn't separating myself from my daughter, and he didn't question it. "We don't want to get in Kia's line of fire, but we've got to be ready to take down the ones that get to close. Kia -- don't you shoot us, got it?"

"I won't," she said.

The tension was tight. Thick. I smiled. "I'm going to need you to cross your heart."

"I do. Cross my heart, and hope--"

She stopped, looked away. Killed the mood I'd tried to set. "It's okay. I believe you," I said. "I'm gonna give you the honors. I want you to start the melee for us."

Kia held the hand gun out, arms extended. She lined up her shot. Closed one eye. Her finger rested on the trigger, about ready to fire.

"No!" It was Gene.

Kia fired, but had jerked her arm. The shot went wild. I spun around.

The hallway was filled with zombies. They were down a ways, but closing the distance.

"Where did they come from," Charlene said.

The eight by the cafeteria heard Gene, heard the gunshot, and knew we were there. Did they also know we were sandwiched between hordes? Of course they did. Their strategy appeared flawless. They'd outthought us all. Son of a bitch.

We were nearly cornered.

"They're fast," Charlene said.

It wasn't the approaching flock behind us. I looked at the cafeteria again. Those eight moved with agility I'd not seen exhibited before. If they had rigor mortis in their animated corpses, there was no visible sign of it negatively impacting their speed.

"Kia!" I said.

She let out two, three shots. She hit nothing. Wasn't completely her fault. The things ran, but normally. Their balance was askew. Heads bobbed up and down; wobbled side to side. We didn't have time for this.

"Back the way we came," Gene said.

"No," Charlene said. "The cafeteria."

There was no time to discuss it. Charlene wasn't waiting for a vote. I couldn't argue anyway. She, again, was right. If we went back the way we came, our two groups might never reunite. Our safety was in numbers. Even the zombies knew that.

I followed my daughter.

She ran at the first zombie and dropped to her knees. She swung the blade as she slid on the floor. She let out a howling cry as she cut the legs out from under the creature, severing above the ankles and below the knees. The thing dropped. Its mouth had been open. Teeth slammed into the tiles and skidded across the floor and left a *splooging* trail of dark, thick blood. The zombie was far from dead, the brain was unscathed. Rattled, but secure inside a decaying skull. The immediate threat, however, clearly had been neutralized.

With the hilt near my ears, the sword's blade pointed toward the drop ceiling squares, I swung and chopped off a woman's arm. I was unable to easily free my sword and thought it might be lodged in its ribs. I let go of the long sword, and snatched the hunting knife from the sheath on my hip. I grabbed a fistful of the woman's hair and yanked her head forward and down. I buried the serrated blade into the back of her neck, felt steel saw across the spine. She collapsed at my feet.

The gun fired. A zombie close to me jumped back several feet. The bullet hole in its face bled. It opened its mouth and moved toward me.

I stepped on the woman's back for leverage and pulled my sword free.

Another shot took the approaching zombie down. The front of its skull exploded. Bone and brain fragments sprayed around me. I closed my eyes, and shielded my mouth and nose with my forearm.

To my left, Charlene held the sword in one hand, and with the twenty inch machete, she cut free the bowels of one zombie, and then swept out its feet with a kick of her own. When it fell, slithering around on its own intestines and guts, she planted a foot on its skull and pounded the tip of her sword into its ear.

If we were not in the middle of some crazy battle, I'd have laughed at Gene. He handled the machete I'd given him like he was French and in the midst of a duel. With one hand on a hip, he stepped and back stepped, and swung the blade out in front of him, cutting into and chunking away pieces of the creature's flesh. It might be his style, but we had no time for technique.

"I'm out!" It was Kia. She held her gun up in the air. Not sure why she did that. I could not recall her firing off more than a handful of shots. Somehow, I'd managed to miss three clips worth of ammo being used.

"Chase!" Allison was at the cafeteria doors. She held it open, waved us over. "Come on!"

"Go, guys. Go!" I said, ordering them to push past what was left, ignore what came at us, and just get to the cafeteria.

Charlene ran to Kia, "Go," she said.

Kia was out of ammo, and my daughter had the sword ready to defend them both. The two ran for the door. Gene and I were right behind them.

I heard the other zombies, the ones that had been coming down the hall. They sounded enraged. Their screams and moans echoed and filled the hallways. The only saving grace, the only thing that kept this from becoming a slaughter instead of a minor victory, was that the other creatures were slow. Very slow.

As Allison closed the cafeteria doors, Melissa wedged a mop through the handles.

A mop.

That was what had kept them at bay before we'd turned that corner. A mop.

"They came out of nowhere," Dave said. "As soon as you guys left. It was almost like they were waiting for you to go check out why the lights malfunctioned."

"They were," I said.

"What?" Andy said, standing between Michelle and Robert.

"Those things fucked with the generators," Gene said. He wrapped an arm around his wife.

"There's got to be thirty, forty of them, Dad." Charlene stared at the wall. "That glass won't hold them."

I remembered going to a rock concert, when being on the floor as opposed to in seats was cool. Only once, did I venture to the front. The stage was set off by a waist-high rail that worked as a fence. Security stood between the two sections; the audience and the performers. Once the main act hit the stage, the force of thousands of people was crushing. There was nowhere to go. My waist was pressed into the rail and felt like circulation was cut off to the rest of my body. Breathing became difficult and I wasn't the only one. A girl by me passed out. Security had to physically move people away. They pulled her under the rail and ushered her away to paramedics standing by. The band actually stopped several times and asked everyone to take steps back, so they wouldn't crush the people up front. While the idea was thoughtful, the safety concerns were lost on the fans.

That's what was happening now. We, the eleven of us were the rock stars. The zombies, our biggest fans. They didn't care that the people against the glass were being flattened. It didn't keep the ones being crushed from still licking and trying to bite through the glass.

"We don't have long. Charlene's right. The glass, it won't hold," I said.

"It's Plexiglas. It should hold. They shouldn't be able to break that," Gene said. "Holy shit."

"Holy shit, what?"

"Gregory. It's Greg."

I looked around. I did not see anyone new in our group. "Gene, what the hell are you talking about?"

Gene walked up toward the lunch tables, around them and right up to the glass, all the way at the right of the wall. He pointed a finger at the flattened nostrils of a man whose face looked like a dog had attacked him. The skin on his cheek had peeled back and hung loose toward his own throat. "That, this guy, he's Greg. Gregory," Gene said. He shook his head, smiling.

"I guess I'm missing the funny here, Gene."

"The generators. Greg did it. He's the one --this guy right here-- that's my partner. You know what I mean? We worked together. Day in, day out, the last several years. If anyone was going to know how to screw around in the mechanical room, how to do some real damage, it would be him, Greg. That son of a gun," Gene said.

"He's a not human anymore, he's one of those things," Melissa said.

The monsters had organized. They'd plotted an attack, and pulled it off. If it didn't scare the shit out of me so much, I'd be impressed. "We need to find a way out of here. Out of the cafeteria."

"And go where?" Dave said.

"We should get my bus," Gene said.

"Where's a window?" Allison said.

"In the kitchen, back here," Megan said. She ran, taking Allison.

"Got a door back there, too," Kia said. "They use it for deliveries. Take out the trash. That kind of thing."

Allison returned. "We're surrounded. I mean--surrounded."

"They are in and all around the building," Megan said.

Dave, Charlene, Allison and I had our weapons. I saw a few rifles. "How much ammo do we have?"

Gene shrugged. "A lot."

"Here?" I said.

"Yes. It's there, stacked in the corner. There's more in the gymnasium, and some by the front office, too. Tried not to keep it all in one place," Melissa said.

"That was good thinking," I said. "What we really need is a plan. Because right now, I can't see a way out of this room. I mean, other than making a run for it, I have no idea what to do next."

Allison walked in a big circle around the room. She chewed at the skin on the corner of her thumb. I hated when she did that. "They breached the school," she said. "As much of a haven as this place seemed, that's gone now. I know I was looking forward to staying here, but we can't."

"We could push through the doors," Robert said. "Shoot a path to the gym. Collect up the rest of our stuff..."

"Not going to work," Andy said, took off his baseball cap and scratched at his head. "We have the fast ones in that hallway. It's one thing if they chase after us, and we have time to run, but pushing through all of them stacked right there, it's a death sentence. I don't see a way of getting through them without some of us at least getting bit. I don't know about any of you, but I don't want to get bit."

"No one wants to get bitten," Michelle said.

No one was arguing. Voices were loud, though. Getting louder.

"We have backpacks," Megan said, "gathered them earlier from lockers and left in the hallways. Dumped the books and stuffed them each full of supplies and stuck them in the dry storage room. Maybe we should hand those out?"

"That's a good call," Kia said. "I'll grab them."

"What's in the backpacks?" Charlene said.

"Each has basic First Aid stuff, band aids and alcohol and gauze with tape. Some granola bars, couple cans of food, and other nonperishables. Perfect to hold you over for a few days, not much longer," Gene said. "Why don't you and Melissa go and grab them?"

"I have one idea," Charlene said. She spoke softly, as if unsure anyone would take her idea seriously.

"What have you got?" I said.

"Gene, you said your wife was on her way to pick you up from work here at the school, right? So where is her car?"

"Right out back," Gene said.

Charlene told us the rest of her plan. It wasn't the best idea, but might prove the only plan plausible enough to work.

CHAPTER EIGHTEEN

It looked like it might come down to a vicious game of Rocks, Paper, Scissors. Gene was an automatic because it was his car, and his bus we were going to retrieve. Initially, Robert called shotgun, but Andy wanted to go, too. Seemed safer if all three went. We figured the rest of us would be safe in the school until they returned.

"You be careful, okay?" Melissa said. She hugged her man tight. I knew she wasn't comfortable with him going on this quest without her. "If those roads are bad, you drive on lawns, you got me? No getting out of the car, at all."

"I'll be gone and back before you know it." He patted her back and rested his chin on top of her head.

"I love you." She looked up into his eyes and kissed him.

"Love you more," he said.

I felt odd watching the exchange. The cafeteria was only so large. I turned away, but it was after the fact, and shook hands with Andy and Robert. I planned to do the same with Gene, but he pulled me in for a hug.

"If we don't return, you watch over these people. You take care of my Melissa." He pulled out of the hug and clapped me on the shoulders.

I nodded, letting him know I understood. There was no use in telling him not to worry, that he'd return, and we'd all be reunited. In truth, the chances of them returning with the bus were not good. Not good at all. He knew it. I knew it. Everyone here knew it. I still had to say something. "You just hurry back. No joy riding with that crazy bus of yours. I'm anxious to see this thing."

"You got it!" Gene laughed. "And you're going to love it. Tell him, Melissa, tell him how much he's going to love it."

"You're going to love it," she said. Her words were not convincing. She barely made eye contact. I didn't think it had anything to do with the bus.

# # #

Kia and Michelle held rifles. They sat perched on the sink counter in the kitchen, just under the small rectangle windows.

"This is going to sound so damned obvious, but when I give the word, you two start shooting. Hit as many as you can in the head. The gunshots are going to attract more to the back of the school over here," Dave said. He made a gun with his fingers and aimed it at his own skull. "Don't stop until there's either none left as a threat, or you're out of ammo. Got it?"

I wished there was more I could do. We only had the two windows over the sink. They were small. Rectangle. Wasn't room enough for more than one person stationed at each.

Charlene stood at the back door, her hand on the knob. This was her idea. She wanted to be part of the execution as well. I couldn't blame her.

"Then, when I say so, Charlene, you pull open the door." Dave pointed at Gene, Andy and Robert. "You three run like the fucking wind to the car. Gene, you have the keys?" Dave said.

"Yes."

"Check," Dave said.

"Sorry," Gene said. "Check."

"No," Dave shook his head. "I mean, *check*. Physically check."

Gene held up a key ring. "Check."

Dave took a deep breath, held it and sighed. He nodded toward Kia and Michelle. "Ladies, start shooting...now!"

Kia and Michelle fired their rifles. The recoil kicked their bodies back after each shot fired. They didn't stop or complain.

They kept shooting. I hoped they were hitting targets. I could hear the creatures. The moaning and groaning was loud, hollow. It ate through me, pierced my skin. I couldn't take much more of it, of them, *of all of this*.

"And, Charlene, now!" Dave said, and she pulled open the door. "Run Gene, run!"

I watched Gene, Andy and Robert flee out the doorway. Kia and Michelle fired more rapidly. Megan and Melissa loaded secondary rifles with ammo.

"I'm out," Kia said. She held out her rifle. Melissa swapped the empty out with the one she'd just loaded.

"Me, too," Michelle said. Megan gave her a loaded rifle, too.

"They're at the car," Kia said, and resumed firing.

I needed to see what was happening. Events being fed to me was not cutting it. It was like listening to a ballgame on the radio when there was a TV right in the next room.

"Robert!" Michelle said.

"I got him, I got him!" Kia squeezed off shot after shot. She leaned back, shook hair out of her face and fired again. "Robert!"

"Dad?"

"I don't know what's going on," I said.

"Charlene, no!" Allison said.

Dave reached for my daughter as Char opened the door and disappeared outside.

"What the fuck is she doing?" I ran around the register, past the ladies perched on the sink, and followed both Allison and Dave outside.

Charlene had her sword drawn and was chopping into zombies. There were so many, too many.

Robert was down. The things encircled him. Gene and Andy were inside the car already.

"Go," Dave yelled at Gene, vigorously waving them off. "Get out of here!"

The engine revved.

I used my sword, too. Allison, Char and I fought the things on Robert. We weren't going to be able to save him. I heard continuous shots fired from the windows. I kept waiting for a stray bullet to rip through my back. I felt that fate was inevitable at this point, and that I was a heartbeat away from dying.

"Robert!" Kia's yelling only added to the confusion. Her shouts would attract even more zombies to the back of the school.

"Back inside!" Dave pulled the remaining things off Robert. "Inside, now!"

I swung my sword around and beheaded a female zombie. Her hands kept reaching out for me. Her fingers curled in and out as if silently beckoning me forward. "Charlene!"

She continued to fight.

"Chase!" Allison called me.

"Alley?" She was not beside me. I could not see her. "Alley?"

"Over there," Dave said. "She's over there!"

I couldn't look around. Charlene and I defended our space, but that did not stop more zombies from closing in on us. Robert was gone, eaten. Dead. We'd managed to throw creatures off of him, but not before he'd been bitten repeatedly. His entire throat was ripped off of his neck.

"We have to get back in the school," I said. It was going to be easier said than done. I didn't want to be around when Robert re-animated. I didn't have it in me right now to drive a blade into his brain. "Charlene, make a break for the school!"

"Not without you!"

"I'm right behind you," I said. I wouldn't be. I needed to get to Allison. She'd been backed up against the dumpster. She used her sidearm and was shooting zombies in the head. There were too many. I couldn't worry about both of them at the same time. "Dave, get Char!"

"I got her!" Dave used a cinderblock as a weapon and crushed skulls with single blows. "Get to the school. Go. Go. I'll get her!"

Charlene was not listening to me. I was not listening to Dave.

Thankfully, Michelle and Kia continued dropping zombies with each shot they fired. I gave up worrying about being accidentally hit by friendly-fire. I *needed* to trust them right now, so I did. As best I could. With that one less thing to worry about, I was able to concentrate on my fight. "Charlene!"

She didn't answer me. Instead, she let out yells and grunts in bursts as she swung her sword, cutting legs off at the knees. She sliced off arms and hands, noses, ears and heads, as she made her way toward Dave, who kept getting closer to Allison.

I followed my daughter's lead, both with wild sword swings, and moving toward Allison.

It snowed large white flakes. The temperature must have dropped drastically in the last day or so, and it felt like twice as cold since the fight started. The wind felt painful against exposed flesh. It bit my hands to the point they felt numb. I could smell winter. Pine trees and fireplaces. Only it wasn't lit fireplaces that I smelled. More than likely it was just Pennsylvania burning.

Allison disappeared from my line of sight; had gone around the side of the dumpster, as if driven further away by the horde of zombies encroaching ever forward. "Alley! Allison!"

Dave held the block in the rectangle holes and spun round and round clocking anything in his way. The heavy grey brick was a ruthless weapon for the bear of a man.

Charlene worked her way closer to the dumpster. She just stepped forward and thrust her blade into whatever was near. Seemed like she wasn't concerned with killing zombies as long as she stopped or slowed them down.

The zombies screamed and roared as we fought them. They were extremely animated. Strong. They kept coming at us. More rounded the corners. I had no idea how much ammo Kia and Michelle had. They were doing a great job at taking out the creatures.

There were just too many. The constant gunshots, the noises the zombies made, the screaming we did as we fought them…it had to be like a giant dinner bell being rung.

"Allison!" I'd reached the dumpster. Charlene and Dave defended Allison as best they could.

"I have her, Chase! Cover me!" Dave threw the cinderblock at the crowd of zombies. He squatted and lifted Allison up over his shoulder. I saw blood flow from wounds on her arm. It sprayed, staining Dave's clothing.

"Let's go, Charlene! Get back inside!" I said. I spun right and left and leapt forward, and jumped back. I let my blade cut into everything around us. Anything close, I cut, chopped and severed. My eye was on Charlene, who was now beside me, and we fended off creatures as we protected Dave on the few yards we needed to cover in order to get back inside the safety of the school.

Then we were inside, door closed, locked.

We were safe.

Except Robert was dead.

Robert was dead, and Allison had been bitten.

CHAPTER NINETEEN

1216 hours

"Chase!" Allison held out a hand.

Dave used an arm to swipe a cash register to the ground before he laid Alley down on the checkout counter. The register shattered on red tiles. I saw fear in her face. I *felt* that fear like a fire inside my own chest. "Hang on, honey."

Everyone stood back. The windows over the sink were now closed. Michelle sat on the counter, her back to the wall, her knees up. The rifle rested between her legs. Megan, Kia and Melissa stood huddled close together.

Charlene cried, silently. Tears left clean streaks down a blood and dirt covered face. Her body shook as Dave placed an arm over her shoulder.

"It's bad?" Allison's lower lip trembled. Her eyes were opened wide. They looked at me, looked around me, and then back into my eyes. "This is bad."

"I'm going to need water. Lots of water? And towels," I said. "Light the stove and find a spatula. A metal one, not plastic."

"A spatula?" Alley said. "Chase?"

Kia grabbed a silver bowl and filled it with water, as Dave tore hand-towels into strips that we could wet and use to wipe up the wound. I took Dave to the side, and whispered, "I want you to hold her down."

"Chase," Alley said, again.

"I'm right here," I said. "I want you to stay calm. Charlene, help me get her coat and shirt off."

I needed to see if she'd been bitten anywhere else beside the arm. For what I had in mind, the water, the towels, we could use those supplies after. The deep breath I sucked in made me wince. It felt like a fist suddenly closed over my heart.

Charlene helped Allison shrug out of her coat, and pull off her shirt. The bra she wore was stained with blood. I poured water onto her chest. The blood washed away. I looked for bite marks. I did not see any.

"Only on my arm," she said. "I got bitten once. On my arm."

I whispered to my daughter, "Heat the end of the spatula up on the flame. Get that metal glowing."

The bite on her arm was severe. It started at the forearm, and flesh was pulled loose up past the elbow. The blood spilled from the wound. The school kitchen was so silent, except for an occasional sob. I heard my own breathing. It filled my ears. "Lie back down," I said. "I want you to hold still. Hold out your arm."

Dave stood at the head of the counter. I nodded to him. He held her by the shoulders.

"Chase…"

"Just do it, Alley." I pulled the machete from the sheath and held it with both hands. The sword was contaminated with fresh zombie blood. If I severed her arm using the sword, it might not help at all when her blood mixed with the infected blood on the blade. This might not work anyway. I only had seconds before it was possibly too late to do anything.

"Chase!"

There was no time for waiting, for talking her through it. I swung the machete fast, hard and screamed when I felt the metal make contact, and chop through skin, and muscle and bone.

Her arm fell from her body. It plopped into the formed pool of blood on the kitchen tiles. Blood splattered. The severed limb was coated red. More blood sputtered from the stub of an arm.

"The spatula," I said.

Charlene removed the flipping end from the flame and handed it to me.

Allison yelled. She did not seem able to form any words. It

looked like she was being electrocuted the way her head kept going from side to side. Almost worried I might need to stick something in her mouth to keep her from biting off her tongue.

I pressed the heated utensil against the stump, hoping it would immediately cauterize the wound and stop the bleeding. The spatula sizzled against the flesh. I think I screamed. The putrid odor of cooking human meat filled my nostrils. I vomited. My stomach bile mixed with her blood and severed arm.

Alley let out a single scream as well, and then went abruptly silent.

Her eyes were closed. The pain must have been too much. She had to have passed out. I hope she passed out. I wished it had been earlier. I didn't want her to remember all of this. It was something I'd never forget. The images were seared into my brain. Seared forever into my memory.

I just kept hearing one phrase replayed over and over inside my head: *I cut off her arm. I cut off her arm. I cut off her arm.*

Melissa and Kia came over. They dipped the torn strips of towel into water and washed the blood around the Alley's wound. I backed away, letting them tend to Alley for now.

"Are you okay?" Charlene put a hand on my arm.

The simple touch was not enough. I pulled her in for a hug. "I thought I lost both of you out there."

I couldn't hold back my tears. I didn't try. I hugged Charlene tight, with my hands tangled in her hair. I couldn't press her close enough to me. I needed that, her close, as reassurance that she was real. That I had not lost her.

"Is she going to be all right?"

"I don't know," I said. "I really don't know."

"You're bleeding, too. Your side," she said.

I lifted my shirt and felt it peel off my stomach. "Stitches must have come out during the fighting. I'll be alright."

"Let me take a look. I'm sure I can fix it up," she said. And I let her.

# # #

I did not see who had done it, but after my daughter led me to the cafeteria area, someone cleaned the mess under the cash register counter. They must have disposed of Alley's arm and mopped up the blood and vomit.

My daughter and I stood at the threshold and looked at Alley, who was still out cold. "Anything?" I said.

"She's breathing," Kia said. "It's steady. But she hasn't moved at all. Her eyes haven't opened."

"I appreciate you looking after her for me," I said, and remembered how, when we first arrived, she'd told stories to take my mind off the stitches Gene had first given to close my deep cuts. I touched my side, and let out a wince.

"It's nothing."

"Melissa, how far away is your house, where the bus is, from the school?" I said.

"Ten minutes. Fifteen in heavy traffic. We're pretty close. About three miles out on McCarren Street, by the hospital," she said.

By the Hospital meant nothing to me. Ten minutes, three miles. That I understood. "How long have Gene and Andy been gone?"

Robert was outside. Had he re-animated? Was he a zombie now?

Dave looked at the clock on the wall by the door to the freezer. "An hour."

An hour. "That's not bad. Roads are littered with disabled vehicles," I said. Getting from 9-1-1 to my kids had been a journey, as well. "It took us, what Dave…days to go just over fifteen miles."

"That's right, it did," he said.

Melissa smiled. It was like she wanted what Dave and I implied to be an acceptable reason for why Gene and Andy weren't back yet. It wasn't. Not really. "I told him not to get out of that car. You remember. So it may just be taking a bit longer for them to get to the house. Once they get there though, he'll be back in minutes with the bus. It's just a matter of getting out to the house. That's all."

"I'm sure it is," I said. "And I can't wait to see this thing!"

This time, Melissa lit up. "It really is spectacular. When he was building it, I'll admit, I did a lot of eye rolling. I mean, we work hard. We're still a paycheck to paycheck kind of couple. He just would dump any extra pennies we had into making this bus. But I never told him to stop. It was his thing. It made him happy, so I just let him. I even helped building it, from time to time, too."

Alley coughed.

I looked at her. Stood there motionless for a moment before I ran to the side of the counter. Kia took a step back. She pursed her lips at me. Not quite a smile. She looked about as apprehensive as I felt. This was going to be touch and go. Alley would need some prescription strength drugs to fight any infections that are associated with amputation. At least that was what I was thinking.

"Alley?" I said. "Allison?"

She coughed again. It sounded like her throat was filled with phlegm. I turned her onto her side. She faced the doorway to the cafeteria where Charlene still stood.

I patted Alley on the back. "It's okay. We're here. We're with you."

"Dad," Charlene said. "Dave, grab my dad."

I looked up from patting Allison's back. I was behind my girlfriend.

Dave came at me. He didn't question my daughter's command. Part of me knew what must be happening. There was something I couldn't see from where I stood. "Char?" I said.

Dave took me by the arms and walked me away from Allison. It couldn't go down this way. Not with my daughter and not with Allison.

I saw Charlene come forward. She'd drawn her hunting knife. "Char, wait. Wait, Charlene!"

My daughter cupped her hand behind Allison's head and thrust the serrated blade into her skull. I heard the knife saw through skull. With both her hands being used, my daughter could not wipe away her tears. Her lip trembled as she tugged and pulled until her knife came out of Allison's head.

I'd done nothing. I didn't save her, couldn't save her. Cutting off her arm, having her pass out--it prevented me from spending last moments together. It stopped me from telling her I loved her. I never got to thank her for…for everything. I failed you, Allison.

My daughter should not have been the one to end it. That she was strong and brave enough was not lost on me, but the fact that she had to did not make it any easier. I continue to fail you, Charlene. Continue to fail you.

Ah shit. I dropped to my knees. Just, shit.

CHAPTER TWENTY

1518 hours

While the others gathered supplies we could load onto the bus and stacked it by the door in the rear of the kitchen, I sat on a table in the cafeteria and just stared at the things on the opposite side of the glass. Dave didn't think it was a good idea. The screaming that came from the kitchen the last few hours had stirred the zombies into a frenzy. I didn't notice any cracks in the glass, but didn't think it made much difference. If those things wanted in badly enough, they'd break through the doors. They just didn't seem to realize that yet. *Yet!*

I was done underestimating the *things*. For whatever reason, they *were* getting smarter. They *were* learning.

Or remembering. Or, was it plausible to suspect…getting better?

"Can I sit with you?"

I turned away from the grotesque and animated death that faced me and smiled. "Of course, you can."

Charlene sat on the table next to me. "How do we keep doing this? I miss my mother and Cash. My God, how I miss him."

I laid an arm around her. She snuggled in close. "I miss him, too."

It felt like weeks, months, but it had only been days since his death.

She cried. Hard. Her shoulders shook. "It's going to be okay," I said.

"It's my fault. It's all my fault," she said.

I wanted to look her in the eyes. I moved away from the embrace, and lowered my head so that we were at eye level. "What are you talking about, honey? None of this is your fault. None of it."

"You left me in charge of Cash. He was shot while he was with me," she said. It took her a while to get it out. Her sobbing made it difficult to talk.

"We've talked about this, Charlene. You know we have. That was not your fault. And Allison was with you. Others were with you. There was a gunfight, and he got caught up in the crossfire. That is not something you can blame yourself for. You have to know that. I need you to understand that," I said. I spoke sternly, but with a soft tone of voice. I didn't want her to misconstrue the words I said by how I said them.

"And Allison," she said, without pausing, without letting anything I'd just said sink in. "Allison wouldn't be dead. You wouldn't have had to cut off her arm, she'd still be alive if it wasn't for me. If it hadn't have been for me. That was my fault. Her getting bitten, her turning into a zombie…"

I was thankful I hadn't seen it, her turning.

"Charlene…"

"I ran out there, outside. You and Dave and Allison, I put all of your lives at risk--"

"Charlene," I said. This time, I used a tougher tone. I needed her to hear me, to listen. "You ran out there to save Robert. We came out to help, too."

"You tried to stop me," she said. "You wanted Dave to stop me."

That was true. "Because I didn't want you hurt. We'd all still have run out there to help Robert. You were right. You did the right thing. You weren't putting yourself or your own safety first. What you did was selfless. I am not mad at you for that. I know Dave is not mad at you. If Alley were able, she'd tell you the same thing. You were not wrong to run outside and help. Not wrong at all. There is no blame being cast. Not by anyone in that kitchen, and honey, sure as shit not by me."

She stared at me. Our eyes were locked. Both of us had tears.

"I want this all to be over, Dad. I can't keep on going like this."

Fourteen, and she was at the end of her rope.

Then again, so was I. "We can do this, honey. We're going to make it through this."

She used the back of her wrist to wipe away the tears. "I just don't know if I want to."

# # #

It was not a super expensive restaurant. I'd made reservations, though. The idea of hitting a Red Robin for gourmet burgers and bottomless fries appealed more to me, but I figured I'd better step it up just a bit. While I'd done a bit of dating since Julie divorced me, nothing lasted beyond a few dates, or a month at most. I'm sure it was my fault. Plenty of the women had psycho issues. Red flags popped up like fireworks for many of them. Still, a lot of the issues rested on me, my shoulders.

It was true I focused on unimportant aspects of the relationships, perhaps put too much emphasis on sex, and not any on building a friendship. Allison was different. I didn't want to blow it from the start. So I changed my game.

I didn't think going for burgers on a first date would have been detrimental, but with her, I wanted to play it more safely. It was not a black tie affair, but I wore charcoal grey dress pants with a matching necktie, and cleaners-pressed soft blue-grey shirt. I had to hit a store in the mall for new dress shoes, and went old school with wingtips.

The table was set for two. We were in the center of the place. I understood which fork to use, and all of that. We ordered the surf and turf with soup and salads. Allison looked beautiful. She'd worn her hair down, and smiled most of the night. Conversation was somewhat forced, although I couldn't remember anything said. The one thing I remember most was making her laugh. A lot.

After my salad, the waitress took my plate with my salad fork. Some of the salad pieces had been large, and I'd cut them up to keep from looking like an animal while eating.

"Oh, wait, wait," I said. "I still need my knife!"

I pronounced it with a hard "K." Ka-nife, and retrieved it from the plate as she'd lifted it off the table.

The whole restaurant must have heard me. Allison laughed so hard, she'd snorted. That embarrassed her. I loved it. From that point on, the date was not forced. I didn't kiss her that night. I didn't want to ruin a good thing. It seemed like she wanted me to, looked a little disappointed when I left her at her front step and went back to my car after a simple hug and a whisper, "Good night."

And now, I helped Dave. Charlene had the walk-in freezer door open. We'd wrapped Alley as best we could in tablecloths. I held her under the arms and head. Dave gripped the legs. We set her down on the floor. It seemed wrong. She deserved a burial. We'd taken the time to bury our lost since day one. Allison did not belong locked away in a school freezer but there were far too many zombies still outside. There was no chance of digging a plot. Not today. Not right now. It was why we were putting her in the freezer. If Gene and Andy did not return, and there came a time when the zombies left this building alone, then I would risk it, take the time, and bury Alley properly.

CHAPTER TWENTY-ONE

1630 hours

"We've got a problem." Melissa panted. She stood bent forward, and rested the palms of her hands on her thighs. "The zombies--they figured out there's a doorway into the cafeteria."

That was the worst news I'd heard in a while. Melissa had been assigned to watch the monsters. We stayed out of the cafeteria as much as possible because just the sight of us kept them agitated. And we wanted, no, we needed them to lose interest and wander the school. The herd was too large. There was no safe way to thin it. "They've what?"

She waved. We followed her from the kitchen into the cafeteria.

I heard it. A hollow thump. "They're banging into the door," she said.

I watched. As one, they took a step back, and then as if one of them counted to three, they surged forward and slammed into the entire glass wall, with a concentration on the double doors. "That is not going to hold," I said.

"No, it is not," Megan said.

"Back into the kitchen, everyone." Dave ushered us through the threshold. He closed the door near where the cash register was. Charlene was at the opposite side of the kitchen closing the other, the one students entered and picked up a food tray before shuffling their way down the cafeteria line for their meals.

"They don't deadbolt or anything," Charlene said. "Just a

simple lock on the handle."

"Push everything we can up against the doors," Megan said. She and Kia moved about the kitchen.

"There really isn't anything. The counters are bolted. The stoves are commercial. There's nothing we can use to barricade the doors," Kia said.

The crash was loud. There was no mistaking what had just happened. The glass had shattered. The zombies stormed the cafeteria.

"Dad!" Charlene had her back pressed to the door.

"We're going to have to make a run for it," Dave said.

"A run?" Megan said.

"We'll be trapped in here," I said.

"There are just as many out there," Kia said, she was on the sink counter, looking out the window.

I could hear their feet on the gymnasium-like flooring, squeaking and sliding as they pushed against the closed door, and pounded on the wood.

"Not going to be able to hold this closed," Dave said. He and Melissa pressed against their door.

"We're going to have to leave all the supplies?" Megan said.

"Yes," I said. "I don't see any other way."

"But Gene's not back," Melissa said. "I can't leave without Gene."

I didn't have the heart to tell her, especially right now, that Gene and Andy probably weren't going to make it back. They'd been gone hours. If they had not returned yet, there was a good chance they were dead, or worse. "They'll find us," is what I said. "If you stay, you're not going to make it. Gene wants you to live, Melissa. He told me so. He told me to protect you when he wasn't here. That's what I'm going to do." I tried not to think about Cash or Alley. I'd sucked at protecting them. "We can't stay here. Any of us. We have to make a run for it."

"Run where?" Megan said. "I mean, we throw open that back door, and fight through the zombies back there, and then what? Run where?"

"We've got to go to someplace where Gene can find me, find us," Melissa said.

"And where is that?" I said.

The door Charlene was backed up to budged. I heard wood split. "Dad!"

Kia ran at the door, arms out. She pressed her weight against it. We needed to move. Now we had a bigger problem. Charlene's door was busted. If we ran, if Kia and she moved, the zombies would be on us fast. The time to run, to get out the back door safely, had passed. Now we had zombies waiting outside, and zombies about to bust into the kitchen.

"Megan, Melissa, get by the back door," I said. This was going to have to be fast. Real fast. "Everyone have your weapons ready."

There was another crashing sound. Dave grunted. "They're getting in, Chase. We can't hold them."

Melissa turned, and like Kia, stood with her hands pressed against the door--pushing her weight to hold it closed.

"It's going to be on three. The four of you, let go of your doors and run for the exit, I'm going to cover you," I said, pointing at Dave, Melissa and Charlene and Kia. I held my sword in both hands, ready. "Megan, when I say open that door, you throw it open, and then you and Michelle start clearing a path for us."

It was not a lot of space to cover. From where Dave and Melissa stood to the back door, it was about twenty-five feet. They had to skirt around counters. Charlene and Kia had a more direct path from point A to point B. Still had some skirting around things, but less of it.

And there would be me, running interference. I nodded at Dave. We'd known each other long enough, been through enough, that he knew I was going to make sure they made it out of the school, that if anything happened to me, Charlene was his responsibility. "On three," I said.

There was no counting.

The door Charlene and Kia blocked split at the hinges.

"Run," I said. "Just run!"

As Charlene and Kia ran, the door fell. It slammed to the floor. Zombies clogged the doorway, shoulder to shoulder. It was almost comical. "Go, Dave, go!"

The door he and Melissa guarded remained closed.

I swung my sword at the first zombie into the kitchen. My blade decapitated the thing. It took several more steps toward me and fell. The two behind it stumbled over the corpse, tripped and fell.

The other four were out the door. I heard something honk. Had to be a horn. It just sounded out of place.

The bus.

I turned and fled. I left the kitchen, pulling closed that door. It was steel. It should hold them for a moment. The fire safety bar across the middle of the door did not take a genius to operate. Once they pushed on it, the door would open. It was that simple.

Bus was not the right word for what sat parked at the back of the school. I remembered taking Cash and Charlene to see the Monster Truck Show at the War Memorial one winter. Beefed up Pick-up trucks with giant wheels and tires rolled over and crushed lined of cars. This…bus, easily fit into the monster category. Cash could have stood inside the wheels. The thing was painted a flat black. The windows were reinforced with black painted steel. The front end was the best part. Gene had mentioned a cattle scoop, like those found on the front of a train. But what I was looking at was an industrial size plow. It wasn't for snow removal, though. The "V" blade sat six inches off the parking lot, and went as high as the front windshield. Overall, it had to be almost six feet tall. Gene was right. It should cut through traffic without as much as a hiccup.

The bus passenger door swooshed open. Gene smiled behind the wheel. "Climb on board, Chase."

The cafeteria door kicked open. The hungry zombies growled as they filed out of the school. I ran and followed everyone up and into the bus. Gene pulled the handle and closed the doors. A gate unrolled, like one you'd see at a mall department store at closing time.

"Just lock those in place by your feet." Gene pointed. I bent and secured the locks as zombies beat at the closed door. "They can't get in, but even if they broke down that door, with this gate down, they still can't get in."

I stood up. Gene could not wipe that grin away if I'd begged him. "You like it?"

"This is the shit," I said.

"I rigged the tank. It holds nearly 200 gallons of gas. Gets about 10 miles per gallon. That's highway. But still, should be enough to get us from here to Mexico, if you can believe that. Andy was able to grab us some maps," Gene said.

I heard paper ruffle and looked back. Andy unfolded a map. "We're going to cross through five states. The fifth is Texas. From here to the border, it's exactly 1,680 miles. Mostly highway," he said.

"We drive straight through, take turns at the wheel, thirty-five hours or so, we can be there." Gene put the bus in drive, kept his foot on the break. "What do you say, we done here?"

"Lot of supplies by the door," Charlene said. "I mean, a lot of supplies."

"A lot of zombies, too," Melissa said.

"This bus has everything we could want, I assure you," Gene said.

Megan shrugged. "Then I say we're done. Let's move out."

Kia and Charlene sat in seats one in front of the other. Each had their back pressed to the wall and a knee on the seat so that they weren't so much sitting, but kind of standing in a way they could face everything on the bus. They both nodded, and Kia flashed a thumbs up.

"I say we roll," Andy said.

"Charlene?" Gene said.

She looked at the school, at me, and finally at Gene. "Mexico or bust."

Gene smiled, showed all of his teeth and then cast his eyes on me. "And Chase?"

I hated leaving the food, and the medical supplies. There was nothing we could do about it. We couldn't risk going back for it. "Mexico. I agree. Let's move out!"

CHAPTER TWENTY-TWO

1700 hours /1680 miles to go

Seats in the back of the bus had been ripped out. There were storage cabinets and boxes of dry food and canned goods stacked by the cabinets, without obscuring access to the Emergency Exit door. Shelves above the two rows of seats housed weapons, an assortment of bats and long handled axes, machetes and rifles. There were boxes of ammunition, as well. Seats toward the middle were removed, and had been replaced with bunk beds, one set on each side.

"Gene, I am not going to lie. This bus is simply outstanding," I said. I stood with one foot on a step toward the door and leaned against a pole.

"It's the shit, right? I told you, didn't I?"

"You told me. I didn't completely believe you. I mean, I figured you had a bus. Why lie about that. But this, no. I couldn't have dreamed it up if I'd tried," I said.

Gene laughed and slapped a hand onto the steering wheel. "She rides real smooth, too. We keep her at forty, fifty miles an hour, and that engine is going to hum the whole way. You have my word."

"Okay, you get tired, need a break, you let me know. We've got more than enough people to take turns at the wheel," I said, as we pulled out of the school lot and made a left onto New Castle

141

Road.

"You might as well try to get some sleep. As long as I'm not ramming vehicles blocking our path, I'll do my best to keep all of you from feeling like human milkshakes." Gene laughed, again. He clearly enjoyed himself.

I didn't think I'd be able sleep, but I wanted to lie down. I think I needed to.

"Are you okay," Charlene said.

I nodded. I walked from the front of the bus toward the beds. "Guys, mind if I crash for a bit?"

No one minded.

The bus bounced up and down the highway. I didn't feel at all like a milkshake. Lying down with that steady motion felt kind of amazing. And while I didn't think I'd be able to fall asleep, I closed my eyes and did just that.

# # #

Wednesday, November 24th, 0108 hours / 1265 miles to go

"Dad. Dad?"

I opened my eyes. Darkness was all around me. "Charlene?"

"You've been asleep a long time, like eight hours," she said.

I got up onto an elbow, and held back a wince. I didn't want Charlene to even suspect how much my side hurt. While I needed to clean this stitched area better, what I really had to find was prescription pills. The cut had been too deep; too long to not have something inside me battling against an inevitable infection. I rubbed my eyes, which were not easily adjusting to the darkness. "Eight hours?" That didn't seem possible. "Where are we?"

The bus wasn't moving, I didn't think.

"Kentucky. Just crossed the border not that long ago," she said. "We kept looking for a gas station with electricity, stopped at this one so we could fill the tank, and use the restrooms. Everyone is kind of busting at the bladder."

"Help me up." I held out my hand. She hoisted me up into a sitting position. I rubbed my eyes. I retrieved my weapons and strapped them on. "You go yet?"

"No," she said.

I stood up. "I'll follow you."

Andy was at the wheel, the bus running. "We're filling the tank, too. Had to go in and activate the pumps from behind the counter. Running a credit card didn't work. We've gone about, I guess, over four hundred miles."

"No trouble?"

"Mostly getting around cars and stuff. Highway's bad, but navigable, really."

"You tired? I'm gonna pee. I just got a solid eight hours," I said.

"I know. Good man, that's good."

"Well, I'll take the next leg of the trip."

"I'd appreciate that. I've only been behind the wheel for a few hours, but it's not natural being up and driving at this time of night. I have no idea how those long distance truck drivers stay awake on the road," Andy said.

I clapped him on the back as he levered the doors open for Charlene and me.

We stepped off the bus and looked around. The area appeared vacant and silent. I didn't like it. The bathroom seemed to be inside the mini-mart. I saw Kia, Gene and Michelle inside. Dave, by the pumps filling the tank, leaned his back against the bus with one hand stuffed into his pocket.

"I see you're awake," he said.

I let out a breath I didn't realize I'd been holding. "I can't believe I slept that long."

"You must have needed it. I slept some too, we all did. Those beds aren't bad."

"You all took turns while I hogged a mattress all to myself," I said, and laughed.

"I'll fight you for it when we get back on the road," he said.

"You can have it. I'm going to take a turn at the wheel," I said.

"Sounds good," he said. He pushed his back off the bus, and stood with his weight on one foot. "I'm actually feeling just a bit sleepy."

Charlene and I walked to the entrance, and went into the store. We stood in line for a turn in the restrooms.

"Bed ain't bad, is it?" Gene said. "Not top of the line or nothing, but I think for a mattress inside a bus, they work."

"They work, alright. I'd have believed it was a Sealy," I said. "I didn't mean to sleep so much. There was no trouble on the road?"

"Nothing, really. We knocked four-hundred plus miles out in eight hours. Not too shabby."

"Not too shabby at all."

"We limit stops like this, who knows, we could be at the border in twenty-two hours," Gene said. "I have some empty jugs on board. Offered them to people. Figured we could have avoided this whole stop, if you know what I mean? Yeah, no one was real comfortable with using them."

"I think an occasional bathroom stop isn't asking too much," I said. No way was I peeing in a jug on a bus full of people. Be one thing if there was a bathroom inside the bus, like on the tour buses, but there was nothing like that on this one.

Melissa came out of the men's room, and Megan went in. When Michelle came out of the women's room, Kia went in. I didn't realize how badly I needed to urinate until I knew I wasn't even next. Gene and Charlene were ahead of me. I bounced my weight from foot to foot, and was a movement away from covering my crotch and crossing my legs at the ankles.

To distract myself, I looked around. I knew Dave and Andy were outside watching the place. The idea of just being inside a store like this made me a little apprehensive. We were all well-armed.

"Still a few supplies we could scrounge up from here before we get rolling," I said. The shelves were mostly picked bare. "Anything edible that isn't open we should take. Beggars can't be choosers."

"I agree with that," Gene said.

Once pee breaks ended, we walked back to the bus as a group. We each carried a hand basket filled with whatever else was left on the store shelves. There were a few tins of sardines, motor oil, baby wipes, plastic ware, and toothpaste, a jar of green olives, magazines, and boxes and boxes of Wheat Thins.

"Let me go quick," Andy said. He seemed nearly as impatient as I had been, like he felt his eyeballs about to float inside his skull if he didn't drain his bladder.

"I better, too," Dave said.

I climbed onto the bus, and got behind the wheel. "Everyone on," I said. I watched Dave and Andy cut across the parking lot to the mini-mart. The others took seats behind me.

"I'm gonna get some rest," Gene said. Melissa agreed, suggesting they'd share a bed.

I missed Allison.

Looking around, yet again, I let out a sigh. I'd been waiting for the worst. Expecting the worst, but nothing had happened. The entire ten minute stop was uneventful, and that, for the first time in a long time, felt encouraging.

"Notice the difference in temperature," Charlene said. She sat in the closest seat across from me.

"It sure is considerably warmer, isn't it?"

"Ah, yeah, like twenty degrees, almost."

"It's about fifty-five out," Kia said. She was in the seat behind Charlene. "I'm from Atlanta, originally. Winters were great. The fall and spring, too, but summer was brutal. The humidity alone was relentless. I'm probably the only black woman to move north for a chance at escaping the heat." She tossed her head back a little and laughed.

"I'm not a big fan of humidity either," I said. I eyed the door. The gate was down and secured. I could drive a stick, but was thankful it was an automatic. "Okay, where am I headed?"

Charlene held up a folded map. "I'm your co-pilot," she said. "I helped Andy, too. We are looking for I-65 South. To get there, we need to get back on I-264 West. Make a right out of here, go a few more miles, and we should hit sixty-five."

"Gotcha," I said. "Not a bad co-pil--"

A gunshot.

The steel-covered windows might prevent someone or something from getting at us, but they also kept us from seeing everything around us. I shouldn't have been inside the bus, anyway. Not with Andy and Dave inside the store. I should have grabbed a gun and stood guard. "Where did the shot come from?" I said.

Gene was out of bed and ran to the front of the bus. "The store, I think."

I craned my neck and twisted my head. I couldn't see either Dave or Andy. "Stay here," I said, Charlene nodded. "Kia, take the wheel!"

I scrambled down the three steps, off the bus, and freed my sword from its scabbard. Holding the hilt in both hands I spun around, but saw nothing. "You see anything?" I said.

Gene held a Glock in each hand. He shook his head. His eyes were open wide, searching the pumps, the parking lot, and like mine -- staring desperately into the darkness that enveloped the store. "Let's get inside and make sure the guys are okay."

We ran from the pumps to the front door. The store was encased in glass. It was easy to see inside, except for the rows of empty shelves making up the mart's four aisles. "Both bathroom doors are closed."

Another gunshot. Glass around the door into the mini-mart exploded. It did not come from inside the store. "Get back to the bus," I told Gene. "Lock it down. We've got visitors coming."

I heard car engines. More than one.

"Chase?" It was Dave.

I ran in through the missing glass, and sprinted for the bathroom doors. I slid on the linoleum to a stop. The guys were on the floor, backs to the empty shelves.

"What the fuck is going on out there?" Dave said.

"Company," I said. I heard the bus horn honk. And honk. "I think we're in trouble."

CHAPTER TWENTY-THREE

I watched two sets of headlights come at the mini-mart, one pair from the west and the other from the east. I could see them clearly from where we were inside the rear of the store, the last aisle by the bathroom doors.

"We're trapped in here," Andy said. "Aren't we? We're trapped."

The bus rolled out of its spot by the pumps. It would never be able to turn on a dime and get close enough to the building for us to make a break for it safely. It would need to maneuver around some, and...

"Where are they going?" Dave said. It pulled up toward the main road. We all watched it from where we knelt behind the shelving. "Where the fuck is our bus going?"

"It'll be back," I said. "That's what they should do. Take off."

"The fuck they should," Andy said. He stood up. "Thing's like a tank!"

I grabbed his shirt and yanked him back down. "You want to get your head shot off?"

I heard tires screech. The cars must have stopped right up front, both with high-beams on and aimed directly into the store. The back wall was lit like it was ablaze with halogen fire. I heard car doors open, and saw giant shadows play across the wall.

"Ah shit. What was it, two cars?" Dave said.

"That's what I saw." I knew he itched to destroy whomever

was inside those vehicles. We never saw who shot and killed Dave's brother, Josh. It had to have been groups of ruthless people just like this: Thugs who terrorized people instead of coming together to fight against a common enemy. In this case, the zombies of a fucked up apocalypse. "Look, we have no idea how many people are inside those cars. Figure eight total, worst case. Behind the checkout counter, do you see that door? Has to lead to the back storeroom. There must be an exit back there. Stay low, stay close, and follow me."

"We're running?" Dave said.

I knelt, like a sprinter ready to run. "Ah, yeah, Dave. I have a fucking sword. A sword. Perfect for fighting slow zombies, but these guys have guns."

Andy pumped his twelve gauge. "I have this and a pocket full of shells. We can pepper the shit out of them."

I wasn't looking for an inventory. I'd been trying to make a point.

Dave smiled. "I have my guns, too."

"Full clips?" I gave in.

"One," he said. He flipped the other gun over in his hand. "And half."

I closed my eyes for just a second, lowered my head. Where the fuck was the bus?

I removed my machete. "When you're out of ammo, we're chopping the bastards up. Got it?"

"Hey! Hello?"

Dave, Andy and I stared at each other. I put a finger to my lips, and silently (and needlessly), *shushed* them.

More glass fell. It sounded like it had been kicked in; clearing shards that dangled in the door's frame. Boots crunched on pieces of glass. My nose wrinkled. A foul stench filled the store. Sweat, urine and feces.

Watching shadows on the wall was all we had. I counted three. I didn't dare sneak a peek. I knew if I looked, my head would get blown away. Wasn't the way I was going to die. I hadn't made it this far to be shot.

I pointed to the opposite end of the aisle. Dave and Andy nodded. I crawled toward my end, the one closest to the front entrance, where the men with guns were.

There was no plan. There had been no time to make one.

"We hear you. We saw you in here. Just give it a rest, okay? Give it a rest and stand up. No reason to draw this out."

"We don't have anything you'd want," I said. "We just stopped to use the bathrooms."

"You have that bus. We'd want that."

"You see a bus out there?" Dave gave away his position. Why the fuck did he talk? Didn't he trust me to handle this? After all of this time together, he should know better than to open his mouth. What was the purpose of us splitting up, if he was just going to blow it right away? We get out of this, I'm going to ask him, because I sincerely wanted an answer.

"No way have they just left you. They'll be back."

The guy might as well have said, "Abracadabra."

I heard the bus return. It must have turned around on the main road, picked up some speed and was now gunning it through the parking lot.

I risked it. I stood. I had been right to. No one was looking at us. The three guys in the store were turned around and watching the bus cow-scooper-obscured headlights barreling down on the store.

"Dave!" I said.

I didn't know where was going to be safe.

Dave stood. He must have seen the bus, but it didn't detract him. He fired off three rounds. His bullets struck two of the men. I couldn't tell if they'd been killed, but they sure as shit went down.

The third guy spun around just as the plow on the bus smashed into the side of one of the two cars. Metal crushed and creaked as the windshield popped, and shattered and rained pellets all over the parking lot. The plow drove the first car into the second.

I heard screams. People had been inside those cars.

If they weren't dead, they had to be trapped with injuries. I couldn't imagine anyone climbing out of either car without at least a concussion.

Dave fired off shots at the third guy, the one who ran from the store.

I didn't know the status of the other two. Dave knew enough not to assume shit. He was on his side of the aisle, I was on mine. We both took cautious steps toward the front of the store where the two men went down.

"Guys," Andy said from behind us, still standing by the bathroom door.

I held up a hand. "Stay."

It wasn't my intent to treat him like a dog, but if he didn't know enough to shut up and just be still, I had no issue reminding him.

The bus backed up, the double doors swooshed open.

"Close those!" I said.

Gene, Michelle and Megan stepped off the bus with a rifles in their hands. They looked bad ass, I'd give them that. I remembered when we'd first met on the street by the high school. Getting off a crashed plane and seeing these guys with their guns was very intimidating. Right now, it would be best if they stayed out of it.

"Get back on the bus!" I said, and pointed with the tip of my sword blade. Michelle and Megan moved to the front of the bus, where the cars they'd smashed would be.

The side of Gene's head exploded; brain and skull and hair bits sprayed onto the ajar bus door.

"Son of a bitch," I said.

Dave reached the end of the aisles first and stepped around the corner fast. He positioned himself quickly into a firing stance with his feet shoulder length apart, both hands on the grip and let off three rounds. Looked like two went into one guy, the third into the guy a little further away.

I rounded the corner. If the two guys he'd shot hadn't died immediately, they were certainly dead now.

Melissa came off the bus screaming. Couldn't Kia or even Charlene have restrained her? "Get back on the bus! Close the doors!"

She didn't listen to me. She dropped to her knees beside to her dead husband.

"Andy," I said. "Get up here!"

Holding his twelve gauge and the machete I gave to Dave, he stared at me with his mouth closed tight and tears streaming down his face. "Get on the bus. Keep everyone inside. Watch out for that other guy. Here, here, give me the machete."

I didn't know where the third guy was, the one that killed Gene. And I couldn't see Michelle or Megan. Andy held the shotgun up as he backed against the threshold, and did a quick peek around the building. "He's over by the cars, checking on the others stuck inside."

"Be careful," I said.

Dave walked up to me. I tossed him the machete. "Don't just leave it lying around, okay?"

"Sorry about that," he said. He looked at Gene and Melissa, and back at me shaking his head. "What the fuck, man."

Andy moved. I wasn't ready. He was faster than I'd expected. He scooped up Melissa and carried her onto the bus. The doors closed. She didn't make a sound. I don't think she even knew what was happening until Andy already had her safely off the pavement.

There was more gunfire. Handguns. "Michelle? Megan?" I said.

Dave crouched, crossed from the store to the bus, and flattened his back against it. He waved me over. "I don't see them."

I heard a rifle shot. They were fighting.

The bus' headlights shone on the wrecked cars. I couldn't tell if anyone was inside either of them. "Michelle! Megan!"

Nothing.

Dave and I moved to the cow-scoop on the front of the bus. I looked around the pointed edge. Both women were standing, and firing.

I couldn't make out their target. "Get back on the bus."

Megan faced me. "There are three of them. They climbed out of the cars. They're just over there."

"I don't care," I said. "Let's go. Come on, come on!"

A gun shot. Michelle fell. Blood spurt from the back of her thigh.

Dave and I came out from behind cover, and ran past Megan.

"Run," I said.

Megan knelt next to Michelle, who was screaming. She writhed on the pavement, threw back her head and reached to hold her leg with both hands. I slid my sword into the scabbard, and squatted down beside them.

"I've got you. I have you," I said. Dark blood sprayed from her leg in time with each rapid beat of her heart.

"My God, Chase, it hurts. I mean, it really stings," she said, and smiled.

"Grab onto me," I said, and Michelle wrapped her arms around my neck.

"I can help," Megan said.

"Get her rifle," I said. "Megan, the rifle."

I saw the hole in the center of Megan's forehead. Small. Round. Blood trickled down her face. She fell forward. Michelle screamed.

Dave grabbed the two rifles. "You have her?"

"I got her," I said.

He opened fire. I don't know if he saw who he was shooting at, or if he just fired blindly into the darkness stretched out in front of us.

We made it back to the side of the bus. Kia was in the driver seat, the door opened. "Get on, get on!"

"What about Gene?" Dave said.

"Get on the bus, Dave," I said.

"We can't leave him out there," Dave said.

"I want you to listen to me. Gene's head was blown off. His wife is on that bus. We're not bringing him on the bus. I don't want to leave him out here either. You know that. You know it. Look at him, Dave. Look at him."

Dave cried as he looked down at Gene's remains. He did not wipe the tears that fell from his eyes.

"Let's go," I said.

Michelle was getting heavy. Hot blood coated my arms, and was wet against my shirt and pants. I glanced back, and saw in the bus' headlights where the two vehicle-corpses lay tangled in a knotted metal mess.

Dave opened fire. I didn't expect anyone to shoot back, but you never knew. I climbed onto the bus first, with Dave right behind me.

The bus lurched forward. I heard the engine grind and groan, but power up and accelerate until the purr was steady and rhythmic. It was the only sound for a few miles, the only sound, until Char spoke up and directed Kia onto I-264 West.

We put Michelle on a bottom bunk.

Charlene was ready with water and some clean rags. "I have a bandana you can use as a tourniquet."

"Thank you," I said. I attempted to tie the bandana around Michelle's thigh. It wasn't going to fit. She was losing a lot of blood. "I need something else. Something bigger, longer," I said.

Dave took off his shirt. "Try this."

It worked. "I need a stick. A knife. Something long."

Charlene grabbed a snow brush. "This?"

I snatched it out of her hands. "Perfect."

I used the snowbrush to torque the tightness of the tourniquet. "Now what?" Charlene asked.

Kia was at the wheel. We droned on and on. "We wait," I said.

"Wait for what?" she said.

I did not have an answer.

CHAPTER TWENTY-FOUR

1202 hours / 750 miles to go

It was my first time in Memphis. I'd never seen the Mississippi. Now here I was on Interstate 40, and cruising through Tennessee. That mighty river was coming up, and in no time at all, we'd be in Arkansas. There were so many places I'd have liked to have stopped. So many places to see. My life had been so limited to Western New York. Canada and Niagara Falls were the places outside of New York that I'd visited most. Sixty miles from where I'd lived my whole life. That was sad and pathetic.

Gene's bus saved us more than once. The thing had the power to push through anything blocking the road.

The mid-sky sun lit the land like nothing was wrong with the world, like people weren't dead, dying or turning.

"We've made good time," Kia said. "You want me to take a turn at the wheel. We'll keep on going. No stopping."

The river was just ahead. There were signs.

"Everyone doing okay back there?" I asked.

"Melissa is kind of a mess. She's still on a bunk, her back to us," she said. "And Michelle is hanging in there. Your daughter has kept up on cleaning the wound."

"We're going to have to get that bullet out," I said. "Can't leave it in there."

"You keep saying that," she said. "We're going to need to stop

154

to do that."

"I know, but not yet."

"When?"

I didn't want to stop. Stopping exposed us to danger. If it wasn't zombies, it was motherfucking bandits. There were seven of us now. Seven. If we were going to stop, it had to be somewhere safe. I didn't know the area, had no idea where it was safe. "I don't know."

"Want me to drive?"

I shook my head. "Maybe in a few hours. I'd like to stick with it for a bit. Thank you."

"A few hours," she said. I didn't reply and knew she was not happy with my silence. "You need anything?"

"Big Mac, fries? Maybe an icy Coke?"

She laughed. "I'll see if I can dig you up a bottle of warm water."

"Mmmm. Sounds perfect."

I saw the sign for the Hernando de Soto Bridge. I knew that it stood just over a hundred feet from the water, and spanned 20,000 from end to end.

I slammed on the brakes. The bus came to a screeching halt. Tires had to be kicking up black-rubber smoke.

"The fuck, Chase," Dave said.

"Chase?" Kia said.

Dave came up to the front. He rested a hand on the dash. "What is it?"

"Look."

The "M Bridge," as it was often called, was overrun with zombies. Six lanes, three in each direction, were swarming with walking dead, littered with disabled vehicles, and looked damned near impossible to cross.

"Holy shit," Dave said.

"Now what?"

"Charlene, you have that map?"

Paper ruffled. "There's another bridge just south of here, Route 55 goes over it," she said, my navigator.

"Do we turn it around, head for Route 55?"

No one said a word. I wanted input. I did not want this to be my call.

"We can plow right through them." I turned around. Melissa was directly behind me, her hands on the back of my seat. "Gene made this thing so that it would cut through anything."

I bit my lip. She was in mourning. She missed her man. This was Gene's bus and I was worried she just felt like there was something that had to be proved. There wasn't. No one doubted the validity of this bus. It was a monster.

"I say we go around," Kia said.

In the oversized rearview mirror, I saw Melissa stare at Kia, as if she'd just unleashed a string of obscenities. "Dave?" I said.

The zombies didn't seem to notice the bus yet. There was time for us to discuss the decision this time.

"We plow through them," he said.

"Go around," Andy said. "We don't need to hurt those things."

Charlene stared at Andy like he might be out of his fucking mind. "Give it some gas," she said.

I didn't know the temperature, but sweat beaded on my brow. I felt it drip from under my arms. "We go around, we could easily encounter the same thing, or worse. I'm inclined to just keep moving forward."

Andy shrugged. Kia moved out of my sight, toward the back of the bus.

"You should *all* buckle in," I warned. For the most part, I'd used the cow-scoop to gently push vehicles out of the way, to clear a path on the road for us to pass. I'd hit zombies. No second thought given, at the time.

I didn't even attempt a head count; there had to be over a thousand. They prevented us from reaching the next state, were a barrier keeping us from getting to Mexico. That was what I told myself as I gently pressed my foot down on the gas pedal. The things were halfway across the bridge. It wasn't that they came at us, as much as they just seemed to mill aimlessly about.

As the bus approached, we gained interest among the herd. They turned toward us, arms out, as they stumbled forward.

"You're going to have to gun it," Dave said. "There are so many, we could risk getting stuck."

"Buckle in," I said.

"You want me to get us across?"

"I have this." I stomped my foot down on the pedal. The engine let out a whine as it picked up speed. Gene must have tweaked things under the hood. This bus had some serious pick up.

I held the large steering wheel in both hands. I switched from the center to the left lane. Seemed like less disabled vehicles, as if most drivers had tried to pull over to the side before turning into zombies. How very thoughtful.

I sucked in a deep breath and held it.

The bus gained momentum. The speedometer indicated we were going nearly fifty. I looked at the road.

The cow-scoop was made of steel. It came to a nice point. It would plow these monsters easily out of the way. I braced for impact.

They looked up at me. All of them. The bus barreled into them, but I saw it happen individually.

The front of the scoop sliced into a woman who'd looked too thin, dressed in clothes that were tattered and worn. Loose skin hung from her face in jagged flaps. Large yellow pus boils oozed on her forehead. Both congealed eyeballs, white, cloudy and lifeless, stared up at me as her body was split in half.

The man next to her was shredded. The scoop caught his feet, knocked him onto his back. I imagined the steel peeling back flesh off his legs, and gut. With a bump, he was gone, under the scoop.

The rest of them I saw differently.

I saw lawyers and doctors. There were construction workers and waitresses. I ran over coworkers, peers. I was crushing fathers, mothers, brothers, sisters, sons, daughters. There were grandparents. Friends.

I couldn't keep doing it. The screams filled my head; resounded like hollow echoes inside my skull. My mouth was open. My jaw ached.

I was screaming, too.

I know I was. I heard me. My voice mixed with the lost voices of all the beings I ran over.

All the lives coming an end.

They may have been dead already. Monsters. Zombies.

No. They were dead. Dead, and gone.

I cut the wheel to the right, and avoided an SUV, and a VW. I knocked more creatures out of the way. They fell under the tires. The bus bounced over corpses. We lost the road many times, riding solely on limbs and torsos and innards.

And I screamed, but I had it. I kept control of the bus. We were safe inside, safe as I decimated the herd, the horde of zombies. Destroyed them.

"Chase! Don't stop." Dave was beside me. He braced both hands on the dash. "We're almost there. We've just about made it!"

My foot must have come off the pedal. Subliminal, or something. I wasn't going to stop. I couldn't. This was a curse. It would be a part of me forever. I knew I'd never be able to bury the memory. Instead, I finished watching the destruction unfold. I would never forget it. These were more images added and burned to memory; more material that would wait to play out in nightmares destined to keep me from ever again getting a full night's sleep.

I used my forearm to wipe away tears, as I punched the gas pedal. The bus picked up speed, climbing back toward fifty miles per hour.

CHAPTER TWENTY-FIVE

2227 hours / 305 miles to go

Any time I think of Waco, all I can remember is the Branch Davidian shoot-out. It took place in 1993. Four ATF agents and six members of a cult were killed. What followed was a fifty-day standoff that the entire world watched. I recall being riveted to my television at home, and it was on at work, even though little to nothing happened during those days, just a ton of views of the infamous compound at Mt. Carmel. It came to a head as the explosive climax erupted for everyone to see. A fire was started and David Koresh, the cult leader, along with seventy-three of his followers, including men, women and children, perished.

It seemed fitting that this was where the bus broke down. Waco, Texas.

Steam spat from the radiator. We'd been riding the bus hard for over a thousand miles. The few stops we took along the way did little to let the engine rest and recoup, if, in fact, engines rested and recouped. Andy, Dave and I stood at the front of the bus with the hood lifted and played flashlight beams over a broken engine.

"Overheated?" Andy said.

"Seems like it." Dave shook his head. "We just add water?"

"I guess," I said. "We should let it cool down before we remove the cap."

"Where's the cap?" Andy said.

159

Dave pointed. "That it?"

I shrugged. "Could be."

Melissa stuck her head out of the driver's side window. "How we doing?"

"Have it running in no time," Andy said. Dave and I looked at him. "What? We can fix it, can't we?"

I bit my lip. I knew shit about vehicles, and even less shit about repairs. I could put gas in the tank. Air in the tires. Wiper fluid in the reserve. "I hate to use up the last of our water."

"We have three hundred, three hundred fifty miles to go, still. I'd rather be a little thirsty on a bus for the next six hours

"Well, this is the radiator right here in front," Dave said. "The cap is, it's . . . there it is." His light caught a cap on the side of the radiator. "We let it cool down a little, add a gallon of water or two, and we should be good."

"If it is just the radiator," Andy said.

"It's just the radiator," I said. "Let's close the hood and get back on the bus."

We were already on Interstate 35. This road led right to the bridge at the border. Three hundred and some-miles was taste*able*, that's how close we were. It was near impossible not to imagine getting across the Rio and into Mexico and everything just being rosy and wonderful.

It wouldn't be.

I wasn't stupid. It just helped to think that way. It helped keep me focused, I guess. Helped keep me motivated to move forward. I had mourning that needed to be done. Desperately. I was holding off as best I could. I wouldn't be able to hold off much longer. My heart felt shredded.

"Back on the bus, then?" Dave said.

"Yeah." I switched off my flashlight. We didn't need to attract attention. For the most part, we were stranded. Sitting ducks. I think we all knew it. No one said it though. Seemed if you left things unsaid, they couldn't possibly be true. Apply liberal sarcasm, but it is what it is.

Once on the bus, we closed and locked the door.

"What's going on?" Charlene sat near the front. She kept the folded map in her hand. "You can't fix it?"

"We need to wait for the radiator to cool down. We'll add water to it, and be on our way," I said.

"How long until it's cool?"

It was warmer in Texas than it had been in Pennsylvania, but it was night time. The sun was gone, so it was still somewhat cold out. "Shouldn't be long."

"What do we do in the meantime?" Melissa sat in the seat behind my daughter.

"Maybe relax," Andy said. It was a lovely thought. Wouldn't happen. Like I said, we were fucking sitting ducks.

"How is Michelle doing?"

"She has a fever," Melissa said. "Kia is back with her now. She's lost a lot of blood. This trip isn't helping. There's still a bullet in her leg somewhere. We're going to have to get that out. If we don't, she's going to die."

I didn't want to see anyone else die. We've all suffered horrible losses. I didn't know how Melissa was holding herself together. For that matter, I didn't know how I was.

We'd traveled a long distance in a short period of time. "We could look for a hotel, or house, and try to operate on her," I said.

Dave sighed. He didn't say a word. I knew what he was thinking, or thought I did. Three hundred miles. We were so close.

"Or we keep driving," I said. "We get across the border and let a doctor help Michelle."

"A doctor?" Andy said. "I don't think crossing the border is going to just fix everything, Chase. I know this is the plan. I can't help feeling like going to Mexico is just something to…do. We could just as easily be headed to California or Oregon, but we're not. We're going to Mexico. I'm sorry. I am. I just don't think anywhere is going to be that much different from here, or anywhere else. I mean, I saw the chaos on the news last week. This is global. This outbreak is everywhere. Those things, those zombies are infecting everyone, man. The few who didn't get vaccinated, or the fewer still that were immune to the vaccination were far and few between. Far and fucking few between. The monsters are fucking spreading the disease. Biting people. Swapping fluids. Who knows how else the virus spreads, but Mexico? Mexico isn't an answer, or a cure, or a safe haven. It's a fucking different country with fucking zombies. That's what it is. That's all it is. And what is worse is no one is working on a cure. No one is out there trying to find a way to turn this mess around. We're on our own. A wall at a border isn't going to mean shit if the apocalypse is raging on the other side, too. And it is. You know it. We all know it. We're all just either going to fucking die like Gene, or we're going to become fucking zombies. Those are the choices, Chase. Those are the only two choices we really have."

Melissa sobbed silently. Her shoulders shook. Charlene reached over the seat back between them and set a hand on her shoulder. I doubt it helped, but at least she was trying, at least she showed empathy and sympathy.

Now it had been said. There was no unsaying it, no unhearing it.

Andy wasn't wrong.

# # #

While it felt like hours dragging by, the engine had cooled considerably in just fifteen minutes. Dave removed the radiator cap.

"Andy can't have those outbursts. Not in front of everyone. You want me to say something to him?" He said. "I think we should say something. He's going to freak everyone out. You know that."

I held the flashlight in place, and stuck a funnel into the radiator. "We're all feeling the stress. I know he's worried about Michelle and Melissa. Those are *his* people. He wants to take care of them. I respect that. I'm keeping us on the road. He wants to remove the bullet."

"We should remove the bullet."

"Do you know how to do that? Because, I don't know if I can." I twisted open a plastic jug of water. "I watched them work on Cash, Dave. I watched the bullet get pulled out of my son, and he still died. He fucking died."

"But Michelle won't stand a chance if we don't try. She'll die for sure if we leave it in her. It's been in there a long time, man. We've got to do something." Dave took the jug and started pouring water into the radiator. "Hold that light steady."

"I don't think I could do it." I thought of chopping off Alley's arm. All measures to help people have ended in death. "You think I should give it a shot?"

"I think someone has to," he said.

"But not you?"

"No way. Not me."

I almost laughed. The situation was too dire. "Fuck it. Fine. I'll try it. But we can't do it on the bus. There's going to be a lot of blood."

"I don't see how. She's lost so much. She might need a transfusion."

I spun around. "I mean what the fuck."

"I need the light."

"Dave, I don't know shit about a transfusion."

"I'm not saying you do. I'm saying she lost a lot of blood. She's going to need more," he said.

More blood. It felt like we were planning out a way to feed a suffering vampire. "We cut into her leg, fish around for a slug, she's going to bleed more. God forbid we nick something and can't stop the bleeding. Do we just run a line of blood from one person to her? What makes the blood syphon off the right person and flow into her? We need to watch a fucking *YouTube* video, like Gene did, or something."

"I really need the light. I can't see shit."

I steadied the light on the radiator. Dave finished pouring the first gallon. "That look like enough?"

"Maybe a little more. The water should come to the top, right?"

"I think that is only if the engine is on."

"Forget the transfusion," Dave said as he opened the second gallon of water and tossed the blue cap onto the street. "The slug, we've got to do something about."

"She's going to die," I said. "We operate on her, she won't make it."

"You think we should wait?"

It was a decision I didn't want the responsibility of making. "I think we wait. We find someone who can help us. Right now, I'm worried more about her infection. And mine."

"Yours?"

I lifted up my shirt, and shined the light on my side. "This isn't looking good."

Dave winced. "Fuck. You have an infection."

"I just said that."

"The skin is so red around that cut."

"It's more than a fucking cut," I said. The stitches were all pretty much missing. Gene had done a great job sewing me up, but there just wasn't the luxury of resting to let it heal properly. "My skin is hot as shit, too."

Dave put the back of his hand on my forehead. I pulled away. "Stand still, asshole."

I let him feel my head. "Well?"

"You have a fever. A bad one, friend."

"I've taken aspirin. I don't want to use up the whole supply."

"Aspirin isn't going to cut it. You're past that. You need antibiotics."

"Thank you, Dr. Dave."

Dave laughed, and pushed me. "Go fuck yourself."

CHAPTER TWENTY-SIX

Waiting for the radiator to cool and adding water did nothing. The engine still did not start. I turned the key and pressed the gas pedal.

"You're going to flood it," Andy said.

I lifted my foot. "I don't know what else to do."

"Well, don't flood it."

I gritted my teeth. No one knew shit about engines. We all took turns throwing out problems. Transmission. Alternator. Battery. Belts.

Charlene knelt beside me. "What do we do now?"

Finding another bus was not likely. Looking for an SUV made sense. We were in trouble. Michelle was in rough shape. She was still asleep. There was no way she could walk, anyway. Carrying her would be a worse idea. She'd have to wait here. Someone could stay with her. "Charlene, Dave and I are going to look for another vehicle," I said.

"You're leaving us?" Melissa said.

"We're coming back."

"It's the middle of the night. Does it make sense to go out this late?" Andy looked from me to my daughter, and over his shoulder at Dave. "You might as well rest. Go in the morning."

Of course that was a far more attractive offer. At this point, I'd pick procrastination over most any option. I was tired of always being on the go, pro-active, defensive. I didn't really want to go out looking for another ride. I wanted the bus just to work.

165

"We could go in the morning," I said, but didn't want to lose time. We were so close. "Dave?"

"I agree. The morning sounds good," he said.

I looked at me daughter. She nodded. "First light?"

"First light," I said, agreeing to wait until the next day. "We should try to get some rest. All of us."

No one looked comfortable with going to sleep. Thing was, we were in a disabled bus on the Interstate. If zombies attacked, we were trapped. I figured as long as we didn't make noise, kept the lights inside the bus off, we should be alright. Might not be much consolation, but there wasn't much more we could do, or that could be done. It was what it was.

And what it was, was bad.

# # #

Thursday, November 5th, 0700 hours

The three of us climbed out of the bus. "Keep everything locked up," I said.

Andy looked like he might laugh. "Ya think?"

"We'll be back as fast as we can," I said.

"You are coming back, right?"

I couldn't blame him. Humanity had suffered a serious blow. Trust was now an issue. With Michelle injured, he must think us taking off and continuing on to Mexico without them would be easier. And it would. "We'll be back, Andy. You have my word."

"Good luck," he said.

"We're going to need it."

First choice, which direction to head. Back the way we came seemed like a good call. At least, I remembered seeing plenty of abandoned vehicles. Whether there were keys or full tanks of gas was another matter.

"Know what? When we find a truck," Dave said, "I'm driving."

"You're driving?" I said.

"When we were in Rochester, you smashed up at least two

cars while we were together. And if I remember what Alley said, there was one or two before we hooked up. That's four accidents in a day, bro. Way I see it, you crashed more cars than you killed zombies," he said.

"Asshole," I said.

And we walked.

The first car we reached, a hundred yards from the bus, had keys. "Don't matter," Charlene said. "Seven of us are not fitting inside that thing."

She was right. "Let's remember it's here. We have to split into two groups, two different cars, we will."

"An SUV will be best. Something where Michelle can lie down in back," Dave said.

"I agree. Beggars sometimes can't be choosers."

Plumes of smoke rose and billowed in the sky no matter which direction you looked. Texas was no different than anywhere else we'd been. Everything was on fire everywhere. You could smell the smoke. Part of it made me feel reminiscent of campfires, toasting marshmallows, drinking beer, telling scary tales to the kids. Mostly, I imagined death, and dying and zombies. Hopelessness. That's what those fires really represented. A complete hopelessness.

"It's going to be hard to get back to normal," I said.

"What bothers me is the zombies," Dave said. "They've changed the game."

"You mean with them learning?"

"Fuck, yeah," Dave said. "Sorry, Char."

She smiled.

I'd protected my kids from vulgar language. It was a different time then. The "F" word was just a word now.

"Do you think anyone is working on a cure or a solution," she said.

"I'd like to think so, honey," I said.

"But do you think so?" she said.

I shook my head. "No, I don't."

The sun rose in the east. Only a few clouds slid across the sky. I shivered. It was much warmer this far south, the chill was not from the temperature. "I feel like we're being watched."

Dave tensed. "From which direction?"

"Not sure."

"I can still see the bus," Charlene said. "Think it's Andy?"

"No." I looked left, and right. Made it as casual as possible. I did not want anyone to think we were on to them. "Could just be me."

Dave opened the door on a pickup truck. "Keys."

"We could take that and the other car," Charlene said.

"I don't want Michelle in the bed of a pickup. She'll be bounced around, and exposed to the elements," I said.

"Could throw a mattress from the bus into the back," Charlene said.

We could, actually. "Not a bad idea. Let's check a few more vehicles. I'd still prefer something we could all ride in."

"Seven people, with Michelle needing to lie down," Charlene said.

"We've been walking for ten, fifteen minutes. Let's give it a few more," I said.

"Ten or fifteen minutes to us is going to feel like hours to them," Andy said.

"Just another few minutes," I said. "Besides, if we're being followed, I don't want to lead them back to the bus."

"So you think someone is out there, for real?" Dave said.

"I didn't see anything. I just, I…feel it."

"Should we just be gallivanting down the middle of the road like this, then?" Dave said.

"I don't want *them* to know that we know they're out there," I said.

"If *they're* out there," Charlene said.

"Trust me, something is out there, and they are watching us," I said.

"There's a van," Dave said, pointing.

I looked for it. I have no idea why I envisioned a conversion van with a starburst painting on the side. What I saw was a white work van, a ladder on top. "It's going to be filled with tools," I said.

"Might not be a terrible thing, we could go through it to see what we want. Leave the rest on the road. Then we do like

Charlene said. We pull a few mattresses from the bus. Throw in supplies. Might be a tight squeeze, but at least we shouldn't have trouble fitting seven people inside."

Supplies. Hadn't even thought about that. No way, we could keep leaving valuables behind. "I like it," I said. "Cross your fingers that the keys are still inside."

"Check it," Dave said. "I'm keeping watch."

I approached the van with caution, each step carefully placed, as if I were on stairs in a house I was burglarizing. I peeked into the front windshield. No one or nothing was inside. The van was empty. "Lots of tools in there," I said.

"Keys?" Charlene stood beside Dave, sword in her hand. She didn't say to hurry. I heard it implied in her tone of voice.

Everything felt eerie. It was day time and there were no visible zombies or people. There were black pillars of smoke both near and in the distance spiraling up into a blue sky and we had the feeling we were being watched.

I opened the driver side door, leaned in. Keys.

"It's got 'em," I said. I climbed into the van and turned the keys.

The engine sputtered. I expected the worst and held my breath. Instead of not turning over, it started.

I saw my daughter bob her head toward Dave and she was smiling.

"Climb in," I said.

They went around to the passenger side. Dave knocked on the window. I reached over to unlock the door. Charlene pulled it open.

"It has a flat," she said.

"Tire?"

Dave stared at me like I'd just replied in German. "What else might be flat?"

I shut the engine and punched the steering wheel. Once. Twice. I should have stopped there, but didn't. Three times.

My fist hit the horn.

It beeped. I cringed and pulled my hand back, as if I'd been burned, as if I'd just touched a hot stove. The horn continued to blare. I only realized how silent we were, everything was, when the horn started to blare.

"Shut it off, Dad," Charlene said.

I gripped the steering wheel in both hands. "It won't."

I hit the horn again. Nothing.

"Open the hood." Dave stood in front of the van.

I looked under the steering wheel, found the release and pulled it. I heard the pop. Dave opened the hood. I couldn't see what he was doing. The horn stopped. I climbed out of the van and walked around to the front. Dave stood there with a cable in his hand.

"What the fuck were you thinking?" Dave said.

"My bad," I said.

"Dad," Charlene said. "They heard us."

"*Who* heard…" I stopped. The zombies approached from the banks. Both sides.

CHAPTER TWENTY-SEVEN

There were far more than a *few* zombies. They came onto the road from both sides of the small embankments. Dave, Charlene and I stood by the van with the flat tire. The sun had barely risen, the morning had just started, and already, I knew this was going to turn out to be another mother fucking sucky day.

It would be pointless to stay and fight. We had to run. The question was, run to where? Toward the bus? That didn't make sense. Away from it might have made even less.

"That car, Dad," Charlene said.

That car. The one with the keys in it. The one about a hundred yards from the bus. It was a good call. If we could make it to the car, we could at least get away from this herd. We could lead them away from the bus, keeping the others safe inside.

"Fast zombies," Dave said. He pointed behind the van.

"The car," I said, and nodded. "Let's go, let's go!"

We sprinted. It was an all-out run. Dave had the lead. Charlene was right behind him, and I was directly behind her. I could hear the zombies fast approaching. I could smell them. The odor of burning homes and buildings was quickly overpowered by a stench of decay. That was not an exaggeration. A putrid aroma of rotting meat assaulted my nostrils.

"Keep running. Get to that car," I said. I stopped and spun around, as I yanked my sword free of the scabbard. I didn't think Dave or Charlene realized I wasn't running alongside them anymore. I needed to cause interference. If I couldn't, the three of

171

us would die. It was that obvious, that simple.

The fast zombies were fast and close. I had only mere seconds to get into a fighting stance. This was not going to end well. I saw no way out of this. I raised my sword.

I saw their faces.

This was much different from sitting behind the driver seat in the bus and running them over like animals. Doing that had filled me with an unexplainable empathy. I knew then that it wasn't the fault of the creature, that they had once been people, and I thought for each one I'd run down, I saw some sort of spark in their glossed over eyeballs.

I'd been wrong.

These things may once have been human, no different than me, but looking at the hunger in their eyes as they barreled forward, I knew the human element was gone, that it had been replaced with a simplistic survival instinct: kill, and eat.

I didn't even know if these things slept.

It didn't matter now.

They had to die. All of them. Somehow, ridding the earth of this infectious plague had to be accomplished. There was no way to coexist with such mindless beasts, even if they'd learned to open doors, and especially if they figured out how to plot attacks. They needed to be completely annihilated. It was unfathomable to believe that God's next choice for a race to rule the planet was zombies. Dinosaurs, man, zombies? That did not seem like a natural progression. I'd have picked cockroaches next, rats even. Not zombies.

I swung my blade. And twisted and turned and swung it some more.

I screamed as I thrust the steel into throats, and sliced off limbs.

The fast ones were on me. I was down.

The smell was more than I could stomach. My throat tensed. Muscles tightened. I feared I might pass out or vomit.

Rapid gunfire erupted. It sounded like a machine gun. The fast bursts were deadly. The sound echoed against and alongside and over the zombies moaning and crying.

Skulls shattered overhead as if detonated. The thing with its mouth open, teeth bared, ready to bite a chunk out of my face was decimated. I closed my eyes, and mouth against spraying brain matter and coffee ground blood.

I squirmed and bucked underneath the weight of the other zombies on top of me, and cringed as something pierced the skin on my leg above my ankle. I suddenly prayed I hadn't been bitten, that something else had broken my skin.

Kicking out and thrashing around, I was able to wiggle free and scrambled to get back onto my feet. My sword was gone. Buried under the mass of decaying corpses, some still animated, some finally fucking dead for good.

I reached over my shoulder for my machete.

It was gone. I'd loaned it to Dave, and couldn't recall him giving it back to me. Motherfucker.

Secured to my hip was the hunting knives. I removed them, and held one in each hand. I took a step forward, and nearly fell, unable to place weight on my right leg.

"Dad! Run!"

Charlene and Dave were behind me. My daughter ran at me while Dave used the assault rifle and fired until the clip went empty.

"Put your arm around my shoulder," she said. "I'll help you."

There was no helping me. "I want you to run! Get out of here! You shouldn't have stopped!"

"We don't have time for this!"

If I argued, I wasted time. It would be easier just to let her help me. She supported some of my weight and that helped. We were able to run.

Dave had killed most of the fast zombies, if not all. The slower ones were still ambling forward, but we had a chance to make it to the car at least.

Running ahead of us, Dave made it to the car first. He opened the door. We were not that far behind and the zombies were not that far behind Charlene and me. It was coming down to the wire.

I felt tears well up behind my eyes, each step caused pain that shot up my leg.

I heard the engine roar to life. The engine revved. Dave closed the driver's door and threw the car into gear. Smoke spewed from the front tires as they spun almost uselessly, as the tires screamed in protest against dry pavement.

The car whipped around and came right at us. Dave spun the wheel as he slammed on the brakes. He brought the car to a sideways stop, and Charlene pulled open the back door. She shoved me into the car, head first and climbed in next to me. "Go, Dave, go!" she said, and punched a fist over and over on the passenger seat's headrest.

"Where to?" Dave said, but wasn't waiting for me to answer. He released the break and must have stomped hard on the accelerator. For a compact, 4-cylinder car, the thing had some balls. It pulled away with heart just as the zombies reached us, as flesh deprived hands slapped at the windows.

"Stay away from the bus. Go past it, just keep driving," I said.

"They'll see us. They'll be watching. They'll think we're abandoning them," Dave said.

"We'll come back for them," Charlene said. "If they're watching, they'll know that right now, we have no choice other than to get away."

She was right. I didn't want to leave them stranded. I wouldn't. They had to trust that we would return as soon as we could.

Trust was difficult. "We *will* be back," I said.

We passed the bus.

I looked out the back window. The zombies were still approaching. It looked like things might work out.

And then I saw the bus door open, and Kia stepped out. She waved her arms. She was trying to flag us down. Did she not see the approaching horde of creatures behind her?

"Dave, stop the car," I said.

"What is she doing?" Charlene said.

"She doesn't see the zombies. She only saw us driving past them," I said.

Kia turned around, as if she might have heard the zombies desperate cries. Her arms dropped to her sides. She went back onto the bus. The doors closed.

Dave stopped the car.

We all twisted in our seats to stare out the back window as the zombies forgot about me, my flesh, us and the car, and were now just focused on the bus and the people inside of it.

CHAPTER TWENTY-EIGHT

"We have to go back," Charlene said.

She was right, of course. Time was limited. It sounded melodramatic, but time was now a luxury I did not have. I wanted Charlene and Dave as far away from this danger as possible. I wanted to see them safely to Mexico, with or without me. "You have more clips, Dave?"

"No."

"Still have my machete?" I said.

He shook his head. "On the bus."

"Take mine," Charlene said. She opened the car door and got out of the vehicle. She pulled the machete out of its sheath.

Dave got out, too, and took the machete.

I had my knives.

"You can't even walk. Your ankle is twisted," she said. "You're staying in the car. Get behind the wheel."

"Charlene--"

"Stay!" She turned to face the bus. "Dave, let's go!"

"Shit," I mumbled. They were gone. Headed into a battle that I couldn't protect them in. I scrambled up and over and plopped into the driver's seat. I grabbed my pants and pulled my leg up. I looked at my ankle.

It wasn't twisted, like Charlene thought. I'd been bitten.

How long did I have? When would I turn? When would the virus consume the inside of my body and kill me? It would hurt, I imagined. Death would be painful. Knowing what came next, while dying, unbearable.

I didn't want Charlene to see me that way.

Couldn't let her.

Turning the car around, I aimed the car's grille at the bus and at my family.

My daughter wasted no time. She engaged the zombies from behind. They'd been pounding on the bus walls when Charlene sliced her blade through necks and severed heads from shoulders.

Her element of surprise worked, but was short lived.

The creatures now knew she was there, and she must have looked more tantalizing standing before them, than the thought of a people inside a locked up and modified school bus.

Dave hacked zombies like he was pushing his way through a jungle trail in the Amazon. Slashing to the left and the right, he cut away limbs, leaving dangerous zombies alive, but considerably more harmless.

The two now fought back to back.

I drove the car at the mob of creatures. I felt like I was in a jousting match. This little car was nothing like the bus, it lacked the cow scoop, and didn't have the brawn and power and stamina to destroy the things. It was still a car, and when I drove into a mass of monsters, I found my new weapon to be highly effective.

Dropping it into reverse, I hit the gas, backed up and switched it back into drive. A second run knocked out five zombies, but my tires were hung up on the guts and entrails inside a cadaver's belly. I punched the gas pedal, and practically felt those innards spray from the spinning tires before I caught traction and lurched forward. The front of the car hit the side of the bus.

The bus door opened.

Andy, Kia and Melissa came out armed with guns.

Their shooting was awesome. The three of them dropped zombies.

Dave used his foot, planted on the chest of a fallen zombie, to yank his machete out of its skull.

It took too long. "Dave!"

A creature grabbed him from behind, tackling him.

I opened the car door.

Charlene was defending herself against two zombies, and the

others were shooting and reloading weapons. Dave needed my help.

I hobbled forward and raised my knife high. I slammed the blade into the back of the zombie's neck, felt the vibration of the saw skip across the spine. I pulled on its shirt and lifted him off Dave.

Blood spewed from Dave's throat. He gurgled and spat blood from his mouth. His hand went to the wound. His fingers were quickly lost in a sea of oozing red blood.

"Ah, shit, shit, shit," I said.

Dave's eyes were wide open. He looked scared. The fear was evident in his stare.

"You're going to be okay," I said. There was little else to say.

"Dad!"

I looked over my shoulder. Another zombie was about to latch onto my back.

A gunshot sounded. I heard a bullet whiz over my head. The new hole in the center of the zombie's forehead was perfectly placed. It fell backward, dead.

I looked to the right. Kia smiled, and nodded at me. Her gun in her hands.

I heard someone scream.

Andy was down. I saw his legs. They protruded out from under a pile of zombies packed on top of him.

Kia and Charlene worked at getting the monsters off of him.

I saw a zombie climb onto the bus.

I knew Michelle was on there. Injured. Dying. She was defenseless.

Dave's hands reached for me, demanding my attention.

There was no way to save him. There was nothing I could do. I held his hand.

He squeezed it. His hand went limp. Eyes closed.

I raised my knife, and closed my eyes too, I didn't want to do this. I opened my eyes and drove the blade into an eye socket. It was the easiest way to hit the brain.

Charlene swung her sword like an axe chopping wood on a stump. The sharp blade cut away heads, arms and chopped into bone with ease.

Kia fumbled with her weapon. She dropped a full clip. She slapped at her pockets as if checking for more ammo.

Someone screamed behind me. I spun around. I placed my forearm on my leg and pushed myself up into a standing position.

Melissa had her back to the bus. Four creatures had her raised up off of her feet. They tore into her stomach with their hands and teeth, and spilled her bowels.

"Charlene! Kia!" We needed to get out of here. I couldn't see around the bus. If I had to guess, more zombies were coming. They'd be coming from every direction. Our cries of pain and anguish had to be like more of a dinner bell than the sounds of gunfire.

Michelle stepped off the bus. She limped toward Kia, falling in line behind the other zombies already after the woman.

"Kia!"

Something grabbed my arm. I shrugged my way free. I took a step and then brought my arm around. The guy was bald. Decaying. Ugly as sin. My hand held the knife tightly. The blade slit the thing's throat. The head bobbled and fell backward. It hung onto the shoulders by a thin thread of flesh before pulling free and dropping onto the pavement. I don't know why it looked like a bowling ball; like you would place your thumb in his mouth and fingers in his eye sockets.

Charlene aided Kia. She cut the zombies off at the shins. They dropped one after the other. It didn't stop them from dragging themselves forward, but their threat was less serious.

With relentless stamina, my daughter fought the creatures and only hesitated when she reached Michelle. Only hesitated, but then cut her legs away and when Michelle fell, she swung as if the head were a ball on a tee.

Kia managed to load her weapon. She fired again, impressing me with her accuracy.

"Get to the car!" I said. "The car!"

I hobbled toward the vehicle and climbed into the driver's side. I closed the door, and backed away from the bus, backed over lumbering zombies. The car bounced and shook, and utilized the shocks more than they'd been tested before, I was sure.

Charlene climbed in beside me.

Kia reached for the back door and was gone.

Charlene opened her door. She got out of the car.

I couldn't see anything. I heard the struggle. Something had Kia. Charlene used her sword, driving it down into something, over and over. She got back into the car. Closed her door a second time.

"Drive," she said.

I didn't ask. Didn't need to.

I drove.

CHAPTER TWENTY-NINE

1111 Hours

We drove in silence for miles. The miles turned into hours.

We needed gas. I got off the Interstate and found a gas station. "Stay in the car," I said.

Charlene did not say a word.

I unfastened my seatbelt and got out of the car. I looked around. The neighborhood resembled a ghost town. I hoped the sputtering of the engine hadn't attracted attention.

It hurt to stand. My leg felt numb. The wound itched. I wanted to scratch at it like crazy. Instead, I removed the gas cap and inserted the pump arm into the hole.

The tank needed to be activated from inside the store.

I shuffled around the back of the car.

The passenger door opened. "I got it."

"Stay in the car," I said.

Charlene stared at me. I'd swear all I could see was anger in her eyes. She didn't respond, nor did she obey. She held her sword in one hand and crossed the lot, entering the store.

The pump switched on. The numbers went to zero. I began filling the tank.

Charlene came out with a bag full of supplies. "They had some bottled water."

"I'm thirsty," I said.

She put the bag in the car, left the door open and leaned across the hood. "Your ankle's not twisted, is it, Dad?"

I swallowed. Making eye contact was difficult, but I forced myself. "No, honey. It's not."

She nodded. Her fingers were laced together. She lowered her head into her hands. When she stood up straight, I braced myself. I didn't know if she would yell at me, come at me, or as I wished, just hug me.

Charlene did none of the above. She got back into the car and closed her door.

I replaced the cap.

I gave the area one last look around and got into the car, too.

We pulled out of the station, and I found a way back onto the Interstate. I closed my eyes against the sunlight. It hurt my head. The brilliance made me think my brain had come loose from the inside walls of the skull and was bouncing around free inside my head.

"Were you going to tell me?" she said. She sat with her arms folded. It was the Charlene I knew very well. The young teenager. Not the warrior she'd become.

"Of course," I said.

"Yeah? When?"

I had no answer. There would never have been a right time.

I saw signs for Mexico. We were close to the Rio Grande. We were almost to the border.

My eyes closed.

I heard Charlene scream. The car swerved. I opened my eyes. She had the steering wheel.

"Pull over, Dad!" She said this over and over.

I applied the brakes. The car came to a stop. We were in the center lane.

"Dad," she said.

The virus was coursing inside me like a fire. Both legs throbbed. My gut and chest ached. My arms felt numb. I pushed opened the car door and fell out.

I threw up, and tried to roll away from my vomit.

I managed to get onto my back.

The sun was so bright. I squinted against the light.

I squinted against the light until all I saw was darkness.

# # #

My head was on her lap. She ran her fingers through my hair like a comb, keeping strands from getting into my eyes. Sweat kept the hair off my face.

"You can't do this, Dad. I don't want to be here without you," she said.

"It's okay," I said. "It's okay."

"Stop it, alright? Just stop it. You can't fix this. It's not going to be okay. And I can't do this. I can't leave you."

"You have to," I said. My throat was dry. The fire was inside my lungs and mouth, inside my entire face and head. I opened my eyes. The sun was behind Charlene's head. She was a simple silhouette. "I love you, you know."

She cried. "You're not leaving."

"Get to Mexico, okay. Get across that border."

I hoped there was something there. Something for her.

"I'm not leaving you. We're going to turn this around somehow. I'm going to save you. I'm going to keep you with me," she said.

The fire in my throat wasn't the virus. It was the cry I held back. The lump in my throat was the pain I kept inside. "I love you," I said again.

"You're not going anywhere."

I closed my eyes.

# # #

When I opened them, I felt shocked. It was day time. The sun did not hurt my head. I was able to see the sun stream through stained glass windows. I was in the back of the church. The rows of pews were filled with people in suits and elegant dresses.

There was a buzz to the day. It swelled my chest. I stood by the back doors peeking in. Candle flames danced all around on stands set around the church. I watched the priest by the altar prepare for the upcoming ceremony.

Julie, my ex-wife walked in from outside. The summer sun was brilliant in a blue and cloudless sky. She was with her newest husband, Donald, or Douglas, or whatever his name was. They were dressed to the T's. Julie in a long and off-white dress that complemented her aging figure.

"How are you, Chase?" She said.

I nodded. Maybe I said something. I couldn't tell if my mouth was working. It still seemed dry, very dry.

"Where is Cash?" She said.

She didn't know. I'd not had the chance to tell her. How could I not have told her that our son had been shot and that he died after surgery? It was going to crush her. It still crushed me, mashed my heart to a pulp inside my chest.

The door that Julie and Donald just came through opened again, and in a dark suit with a crisp pressed white shirt and necktie was Cash.

"Hey, Mom, Dad," Cash said.

Cash.

He was dead. I buried him. I'd held him, and placed him in a hole I'd dug in the ground.

I dropped to my knees. I spread my arms wide and he ran into them. "You look so handsome," I said.

"Thank you," he said, pulled out of the hug and fixed the knot on his tie.

I still wanted to hug him. I didn't want the embrace to be over. Not yet, not while he was here. With me.

"Have you seen, Charlene? She looks beautiful." My ex-wife was smiling. How could she look so happy?

Something was wrong.

"We're ready," the priest said, suddenly standing behind me. "Mr. McKinney, when the music starts, you may proceed down the aisle with your daughter."

I nodded.

The music?

"Good luck," Julie said. She and her husband disappeared into the church. I watched them walk to the front of the church and sit in the second row of pews.

What was this?

"I'm ready, Daddy."

I turned around. Charlene stood behind me. She was in a beautiful white wedding gown. The train rolled out for several feet behind her. "You look beautiful."

She blushed, dropped her eyes, as if embarrassed. "I'm so nervous. I can't believe this is really happening. This is a day I've dreamed about since I was a little girl."

She was a little girl. How was she getting married? She was fourteen. Did I approve this? Did her Mom?

"Honey, you're going to be a wonderful wife, and live a happy life. A happy-ever-after life."

"Do your really think so?"

"Baby, I know so," I said. I mentally squeezed my mind, searching for memories of the man she was about to marry. I could not even conjure up an image of what he looked like. Not his name, what he did for a living. Nothing. Not a thing.

I wasn't ready for this. This was my baby. She might be a wonderful wife, but was I ready to let her go? She was fourteen. Only a kid, a teenager. She had so much, so many other things to do yet, to look forward to…

"It's time," she said. "Will you lower the veil?"

I gave her a gentle kiss on her lips, and then just looked into her eyes. "I love you. You know that, honey, don't you?"

"I love you, too." She wiped tears from her eyes. "You're going to make me mess up my makeup."

"No crying," I said. I lowered the veil over her face. It hid her beauty.

An organ played.

The wedding march began. We took slow practiced steps down the aisle. I felt people staring at us, but I did not look around. I stared at the priest and the man with his back to me at the head of the church; the man she was to marry. The man who'd taken my little girl away from me.

The procession took forever. Each step we took did not bring us any closer to the front of the church.

But then, like a snap of a finger, we were there. In front of the priest.

I raised the veil. I again gave her a gentle kiss and stepped back.

I stepped back and screamed.

The man she was to marry stared at me. He was missing an eyeball. Green-grey flesh peeled from his forehead and cheeks. A gaping mouth with less than a handful of teeth set into receded gingivitis-ridden gums.

I spun around.

The church was filled with zombies who were dressed amazingly, seated in the rows and rows of pews.

Now they stood and shuffled out of the pews, and slowly made their way toward me, toward my daughter.

"Run, Charlene! Run!" I said.

Charlene grabbed my hand.

Her skin was green and decaying. She opened her mouth and groaned.

I closed my eyes and screamed.

#

Charlene was beside me, smiling. Her hair was done in braids. She leaned over and kissed my cheek.

"We made it," she said. "You made it."

What had I missed? How was this possible? How?

I looked around. This was still not Mexico.

This was Rochester. We were in my apartment. We were in my living room.

There was my TV. My couches.

"Charlene, I don't understand?"

"You're okay. Everything is going to be okay. I love you, Daddy. I love you."

I opened my mouth, trying to speak. I wanted to say, "I love you, too."

What I said, and what I heard were two different things.

I did not hear: I Love You.
Instead, I heard a growl. A groan. A moan. A cry.
I tried again, harder this time.
A grow. A groan. A moan. A cry.
"I love you, Daddy. I love you!"
Why was she crying? Why?
I reached for her, fingers beckoning her closer, and closer . . .

EPILOGUE

I couldn't just leave things like this. I couldn't.

He deserved better. Much better.

He wasn't just a great man. This was my father.

His cries cut into my soul.

His moans tore at my heart.

To the left was Mexico. The border.

I backed away from my father as he struggled to his feet, and climbed into the car. I drove away from him.

I drove several yards and stopped.

He was in my rearview mirror. He stood there, still reaching for me.

"Dad," I whispered.

I climbed out of the car. I stood and waited.

He came for me. Each step he took pained me. Crushed me.

It wasn't him. Not any longer. It wasn't my father.

I sucked in a deep breath and strode full of purpose in each step I took toward him. I raised my sword.

His arms outstretched; fingers curling and uncurling as if calling me closer and closer..

I swung the sword high, and fast and hard.

As the blade connected with the side of his neck, I closed my eyes and turned away before I saw something I'd never be able to un-see. I slid the blade across his flesh as I spun, and regretted being able to feel the blade shred with a jagged cut.

And then I walked toward the car, and past it...and kept on walking.

#

The sign said *Mexican Border*.

I could hear the river. It ran strong and fast.

There were cars all over the place, clogging the way out of this country and into the next.

Dad wanted us to reach Mexico.

We'd done it. Well, I'd done it.

I'd do it, if only for him.

I wasn't sure this was where I wanted to be, though.

My home was nearly 2,000 miles in the opposite direction.

Not a few hundred yards in front of me.

For my dad, I would cross into Mexico. Maybe it would turn out to be the perfect sanctuary. Maybe I would be safe. Maybe they didn't have the zombie problems America faced.

Maybe there was a new beginning waiting for me on the other side of that wall.

I wouldn't know until I crossed over and saw for myself.

The problem was, I kept thinking about what we'd learned so far. The zombies did not like the rain. Mexico did not get much rain. Ever. The zombies learned. They might never be smart (again), or figure out complex problems, but they did learn. If the things were decaying from the inside out, then maybe, just maybe this nightmare would end on its own. Eventually.

My name is Charlene McKinney.

Char.

In a few short weeks, I'd lost everything important in my world: my mother, my brother, my father.

I'd lost everything *except* the anger that stirred inside me. I had my sword, machete and knives. I had a fire inside me. I wanted answers. I wanted revenge. I knew it might be wrong, but I wanted to kill every last zombie on earth. Maybe I'd start that in Mexico . . . Maybe I'd go somewhere else and settle the score . . .

I turned around, and gave the USA one final look . . .

. . . The End . . .

Author's Note

While Butler County is an actual county in Pennsylvania, for creative reasons I took many liberties with the physical attributes. With 14 movies filmed in this county, including but not limited to, *Night of the Living Dead* (1968), *The Crazies* (1973), *I Am Number Four* (2011), and *The Avengers* (2012), I wanted to include this location in the mix of my own zombie trilogy. If any harm was caused, mistakes made, I apologize as none was meant.

Special Thanks

I want to thank Adrian DeJesus, JoAnne Doud and Linda Tooch, my beta readers; Gary and everyone at Severed Press for all the work put into bringing The Vaccination Trilogy to life, and most importantly, all of the readers who have helped to make the series an Amazon Best Seller. Without my readers, my writing stories is pointless. Thank you, everyone. Your continued support means the world to me.

www.philliptomasso.com / phillip@philliptomasso.com
@P_Tomasso

Other Titles by Tomasso

Evacuation
Vaccination
Sounds of Silence
Pulse of Evil
Pigeon Drop
Convicted
The Molech Prophecy (as Thomas Phillips)
Adverse Impact
Johnny Blade
Third Ring
Tenth House
Mind Play

Forthcoming

Riverbed Treasure Island: A Zombie Novel

About the Author

Phillip Tomasso is the award winning author of numerous novels, and short stories. He works full time as a Fire/EMS Dispatcher at 911. He lives in Rochester, NY with his three children, dog, Fettuccine, and cat, Luca. He is always at work on his next tale.

Praise For VACCINATION

"I loved this book because of the concept; zombies didn't just appear after somebody woke up in a hospital bed! The group of survivors were believable, and I loved the fact that they weren't perfect. Highly recommended." – D.A. Wearmouth, bestselling author of First Activation

"VACCINATION is a thrill a minute. Narrated in a gritty noir voice, Phillip Tomasso drags you into a zombie outbreak face first and doesn't let you go until you've ripped your fingernails off clawing for help. Smart, intense and damn right frightening, VACCINATION is a must for any zombie fan."– Max Booth III, author of Toxicity

"It's hard not to get emotionally attached to the small group of survivors and root for them despite their personal flaws. It's pretty much impossible to describe the end without giving away too much. I'll just say that it was a great twist. Whether you are new to zombie fiction or have been a fan for years, I'd tell you to check this one out. It's a great read." – Ian McLellan, Zombie-Guide.com

"Tomasso created a Zombie book that seems all too possible! This book kept me wired tight from the beginning until the very end. If you like awesome adventure, and vivid storytelling, then you will LOVE Vaccination! 5 BIG Stars!" – Cedric Nye, author of The Road to Hell is Paved with Zombies

"There's a bit of a cliff hanger at the end of the book, which left me wanting more. I'm anxiously awaiting the publication of the second book. If you're looking for a great zombie book, then I highly recommend you grab a copy of Vaccination. Props to Phillip Tomasso for writing this fantastic zombie novel!" – J. Cornnell Michels, author of Jordan's Brains

"Tomasso explores a humanity left dormant in the infected with graceful elegance. While we get glimpses into that unexpected possibility throughout the book, I would have loved digging deeper down that rabbit hole and see what he would have gifted us with. Simply put, however, VACCINATION is on fire!" — The Bookie Monster

Praise for EVACUATION (Book 2)

"Evacuation is a great read. A taut thriller of a zombie book that is wonderfully violent while continuing a great story about a guy who is simply trying to keep his kids safe during the absolute worst of times. It is fast paced and full of action, but also contains a few scenes that are gut-wrenching to go along with all of the gore and tension." Ian McClellan, Zombie-Guide Magazine

"Tomasso is a warmhearted writer with an edge. Evacuation is as much emotional and compassionate, as it is horrific and ruthless . . . Evacuation ends in such a way that readers are left with no other option than to read the final installment. It left me with a buildup of anticipation, and questions that must be answered." Shana Festa, The Bookie-Monster Review

"This book was better than the first. While it was still fast paced and zombie filled, it was also filled with many emotions, not only felt by the characters in the book but by you the reader. The author made you feel scared, nervous, [it made you] want to scream you were so mad, and the ending was filled with sadness and left you crying and waiting to find out what happens next . This book brought you even closer to the main characters." MLP, Amazon

"A very entertaining zombie story. The interrelationships between characters are surprisingly deep with an unanticipated moral theme that gives this book a deeper and more moving character than most. Very well written engrossing and moving. If you are thinking about reading it I say go ahead." LGreen, Amazon

"Phillip Tomasso is one of my favorite writers & this book certainly didn't disappoint . . . If you're looking for a really excellent ZA book, then read this series. I promise you won't regret it! I'm waiting impatiently for the sequel!" ZAreader, Amazon

"OMG loved this book. Can't wait for the next one. Makes you think if we could all stick together if something like this was to happen. Thanks for writing these books. Please keep writing." Amanda Simmons, Amazon

"A great spin on the tried-and-true zombie tale with non-stop action. I couldn't put it down! Can't wait for the 3rd book!" Tony Bartosiewicz, Amazon

"Very fun series to read. I'm a firefighter and paramedic so to see this group is fun, can't wait for the last one to come out!" Roam, Amazon

Praise for Phillip Tomasso

"This is different … confident, addictive storytelling, great characters, and an intriguing plot. You'll read it fast but remember it for a long time. " —Lee Child, bestselling author of One Shot and the Jack Reacher series

"(Tomasso) takes the standard fare of the private investigator genre and adds twists and turns to make it anything but standard. Tomasso's writing is crisp and clear … thoroughly enjoyable." —Joseph Nassise, author of Internal Games and King of the Dead

"Phillip Tomasso understands what drives people who live on the edge. His characters are three-dimensional and they engage your sympathy and your anger. . ."— William Meikle, author of Night of the Wendigo and The Midnight Eye Files

"I have a selection of authors that I turn to when I need a break from Fantasy and Phillip Tomasso has just become one of them." —The Eternal Night Magazine

"Phillip Tomasso breathes new life into an old genre – an EXCELLENT read!" —M. R. Sellers, Author of In the Bleak Midwinter and Never Burn a Witch

"Tomasso weaves a fantastic tale of supernatural proportions in Third Ring. This book keeps you at the edge of your seat, makes you question what you really believe, and entertains, all at the same time. I enjoyed reading this novel because it had just the right amount of characterization to make me feel like I know Tartaglia (the protagonist) but not so much that it took away from the plot." —John Mirak, Jr., author of Time Stand Still and Soft Case

"Tomasso has a hit with his Nick Tartaglia series. His writing is real and flows just the way a detective novel should … THIRD RING is a frightening ride, full of twists and turns. But when the ride is over, all you want to do is buy another ticket and go again." —Nancy Mehl, author of Unbreakable and Inescapable

" . . . This guy is GOOD! . . . The characters are terrific and I can't think of anything better on a cold winter's night than another Phillip Tomasso novel . . . Well done!" —Thom Racina, best-selling author of Hidden Agenda, Secret Weekend and Deadly Games

"Tenth House is fast-paced, super-scary, and supernatural. Mr. Tomasso writes thrills with a twist!" —Sarah Lovett, author of Dantes' Inferno and Desperate Silence

"Tenth House is meticulously detailed in both setting and character depth. The story will pull you in, shake you about, disturb you, keep you guessing and always wanting more. It delivers!" —Keith Rommel, BookReview

"Tenth House is a brilliant concoction of suspense, thrills, action, and love all mixed into a book you won't want to put down!" —Amanda Mueller, MyRochester.com

"Phillip Tomasso's supernatural tale develops three-dimensional characters for a different style of detective series ... where the unexpected prevails." —N.B. Leake, Write Time Write Place

"Fast-paced and deftly told—Tomasso knows his craft." —Olivia Boler, author of Year of the Smoke Girl and The Flower Bowl Spell

"...I look forward to more by this talented author in the future." —Tracy Farnsworth, The Romance Readers Connection.com